Future Sins Volume Two

S. A. Wooderson

Martin in the Woods Publishing

Contents

Sloth: 1

1. Slowest of All the Peoples   2

2. Steve the Sloth   31

Lust: 50

3. Sex Tourist   51

4. NightBlind   67

5. HuMan   79

6. Troll Hunt   95

7. Prostitute 732   100

8. Human Contact   107

Gluttony   118

9. The Traveler   119

10. Tsunami   126

Pride   135

11. AlOne   136

12. Jacob's Ladder Down   143

13. The Elevator's Arrogance   179

Sloth:

Chapter One

Slowest of All the Peoples

"And so it was said and so it was done that our God, the God, the only God, slept and rested. For he was finished with the creation of the universe, and it was time for him to rest. And there on the edge of the universe he slept, and his universe continued on without him. He was finished creating all that could be and all that was.

"For it was said that God, the God, creator of all we know and can see, was the God of Creation and Destruction, and that in his dreams he continued to bless and care for his people, the people of the million worlds, the ones blessed with his gift of a rich universe with infinite variety.

"And yet all infinites are not equal, and this universe is not infinite nor equal to the universes before. But God in his wisdom will grant us serenity and continued existence and we pray that he may slumber for infinite ages.

"For the ages of man are short and the time of God is long. Blessed Be."

"Blessed Be," the congregation repeated and stood up to walk outside.

Bryan yawned. He'd heard it all before. He gave a nod and walked out of the church with his family. The heat of the circling suns hit him, and he stumbled blindly towards his family's wagon. Three more weeks. Three more weeks, he told himself, and he would go to the Academy. Amy was standing by the wagon scratching Perry, their lead horse, between the ears.

"Why, hello, Bryan," she said smiling.

He squinted and smiled.

"Why, I thought you might be ignoring me," she said, twirling her skirt a little, "and after I went to all this trouble to make a new dress. I look nice, don't I, Bryan?"

He yawned again. It had been a long night trying to read all the required reading before the semester started. He'd gotten through the *Basics of Quantum Thermal Induction* but fallen asleep before he could start *Gravity Wells and Time Displacement*. He was so far behind; all the other cadets would be coming from wealthy space-faring planets, and he was only getting in because of the affirmative action edicts. And besides which, Farmtyn as a member of the Federation needed some representation in the Federation and it was hard to find anyone qualified on a planet that valued a good plow horse over a good education.

"Well, don't trip over yourself giving me a compliment," Amy continued.

"Sorry, I am just tired. You look nice."

"What are you up to this afternoon, Bryan?" She tilted her chin down and lifted her eyes to look at him. He'd seen girls do that a lot lately. Seemed like as they got older they just held themselves all funny like. Marybel at the ice cream store last week had that same odd expression, and she'd expected him to buy her an ice cream, which didn't make sense at all when her poppa had given her enough money for one.

"I need to study some more, Amy; I only have a week till basic training starts and I need to leave."

"You aren't really going, are you, Bryan?" It was about the same question Marybel had asked with that same weird tone. Bryan was starting to realize one of the truest expressions was true. Women were unfathomable.

"Of course I am going. I am going to be the first Space Explorer ever to come from Farmtyn and I am going to go all the way out to deep space, to the edge of the known universe, and see what's there."

Amy started to cry. "There's nothing there but God, Bryan. Why don't you just stay here with us?"

Bryan was happily distracted by his older brother Martyn. "Hello, Amy. Don't you look nice."

"Yes, I do. Thank you for noticing, Martyn." She smiled and dipped her chin again. Martyn was only a year older than Bryan, but he seemed to have worked out better what to say to strange girls.

The rest of the family had stopped to talk to the pastor, but they all approached, having finished their greetings. As the middle child of twelve, Bryan wondered if he'd actually be missed when he was gone.

By the time he'd collected the eggs and come in for dinner he felt like he was too tired to notice what he was putting in his mouth. He looked down and realized the bread and beans were gone and he still had to eat the vegetables.

"Bryan."

"Yes, Poppa."

"How did you fare on the study last night, son?"

"I am finding it difficult."

"Well, if God wills it you will get in." If God wills it was Poppa's answer to everything. Bryan shoveled down the rest of the food and only two plates of milk pudding and asked to be excused to study. His mother looked to his father and when Poppa nodded, he went back to his room. It wasn't often he was alone there. Normally the other four boys would be in various stages of sleeping, snoring, dressing, or wrestling. He picked up the next book and fell asleep with it on his face before his brothers came to bed.

Three weeks of stressing and studying and he'd never given any thought to the actual leaving. The actual leaving was something he was sure would be fun and exhilarating and he hadn't thought how it could be sad. Poppa and Martyn had taken him to the launchpad and there stood the rocket. The horse and cart parked at the space station seemed strange, perhaps as strange as a poor country boy heading off to study at the Space Academy. Bryan waved and smiled, and he saw his father put his arm up straight in greeting, an acknowledgment of his departure but not an acceptance of it. Bryan rubbed some dust from his eye, turned and walked into the rocket. This was his adventure, and he was going to enjoy it.

"Buckle up," said the pilot. "This is a short 4-hour flight so you will remain seated. Please do not travel about the cabin. If you need to get out of your seat to visit the toilet facilities, please hold on to the rails provided. This vessel has no artificial gravity field so you will experience weightlessness. If you feel in any way unwell push the red button on your seat and lean forward into the face receptacle provided."

Bryan figured the face receptacle was the silicone looking thing in front with a tube. He'd read about those. It was pretty basic; just a soft resting place that would vacuum away vomit but would also take the passenger's vital signs and provide medication or anesthesia should the passenger request or require it. They had invented it in the beginning days of space travel when so many people had gotten ill or been hysterical while traveling. Most people chose to sleep away their voyage, but Bryan wanted to enjoy every minute.

He looked around. The rocket only had 8 passengers. Farmtyn inhabitants did not travel. They only had a regular rocket service to ship their grain off world to the nearest space station. That was where they were going. He motioned for the hologram screen to open and selected the screen to show the route as seen by the rocket's exterior cameras.

The other 7 people in the rocket were 4 officials from the station, and a family of pilgrims dressed in yellow robes traveling to visit the Shrine of the God of Creation. Hundreds of years ago it had been set up so pilgrims could go and look out onto the stars through a telescope. They would look out to the edge of the known universe and come back to tell everyone about the mightiness of God. It was an expensive trip and the family consisted of an old couple. The husband was dried and wrinkled in a way that only came with extreme age. The wife was shrunken and shriveled, with the skin of a larger woman hanging from her neck and arms. Their son was large and stout in a way that denoted prosperity. He was also obviously terrified, his face florid and his eyes sunken into his trembling visage. This was the one trip of their lifetime, saved for, prayed for, planned for, and it was obvious that now it was upon them, all three of them were wishing they weren't there. The rocket hadn't finished turning on its motors before all three had pushed their faces deep into the face receptacle and nodded off to sleep.

The pilot walked down the body of the ship and checked that everyone was buckled in. She smiled at Bryan and handed him a candy. "If you suck on this the altitude change won't affect your ears as much. Now remember, just hold on. And there is no shame in using the tranquilizer available in the face mask."

"I'm going to be a space explorer. I'm going to the Academy. I want to be awake."

"Ok, love," she said and walked away to the next person. Then went back to the cockpit. Once, she had been as enthusiastic as that little boy. Now she ran a small unimportant rocket on its daily grain run from the space station to a small farming community not worthy of a spaceport. She didn't want to crush the kid's dreams but not everyone who went to the Academy became a space explorer.

Bryan could feel the motors starting from the vibrations through his feet. Then the rocket tipped upward, and his chair was pointing towards the sky. The soft silicone material held him firmly and the straps held him back as the thrusters turned on and the ship shot up. He looked at the holovision. He was leaving Farmtyn behind. His father was still there, on the grass near the launch site. He looked so small. His brother looked taller, then Bryan realized his father was on his knees praying.

The rocket took off and Bryan felt himself being squashed into the silicone seat, the air crushed from his lungs and his limbs immovable. He wanted to lean forward into the face receptacle, but it was a little too far away to reach. So he sucked on the candy the pilot had given him and then *pop*—he felt them leave the gravitational field of Farmtyn like a sudden joy. The pressure was gone, the tension he had unconsciously been holding in his jaw relaxed, and his whole body floated in its silicone cushion. He gave a quick thank you to God and reveled in the sensation.

This was the moment he'd waited for all his life, and he laughed. The four officials who were seasoned travelers turned to look at him and he knew instantly who they were by their reaction to his joy. The oldest man smiled with the warm recollection of his own childlike joy; the man next to him snarled at being disturbed as he looked up from reading his holovision. The tiny woman looked at him with the kind of affection mothers give their children, while the larger woman sat writing a report looked up teeth clenched, not noticing him at all, just trying to focus on something other than where she was. She was obviously not a fan of rocket travel.

Farmtyn quickly became a small ball behind them. Bryan had always known he lived on a small ball floating in space but somehow to see it made it real. He was really in space. He was really going to the Academy. It hadn't been real before that.

As soon as the pilot announced that it was possible to float about the cabin, he released the seatbelt as the holovision safety video directed. He floated upwards grabbing the rail, and using both hands pulled himself along the rail to the toilet facilities. He went in and the door shut. He was in a small room with a silicone waste receptacle. He pulled down his pants and attached it. When he was done the device retracted, and he put his pants on as well as possible. Doing up buttons wasn't as easy without a center of gravity, and he decided that as soon as he was off-world he would buy some magnetic opening and closing clothes for his next flight.

By the time they approached the space station, with the arrogance of youth and testosterone, Bryan felt like he had mastered space travel. The docking of the ship to the station was a smooth and easy transition. And then the artificial gravity of the spinning station hit him and after the hours of weightlessness he felt like he was being crushed into the rocket seat. He suddenly appreciated the squishy silicone chair.

The most scared of the dignitaries unbuckled first, throwing herself out of the seat and towards the exit door, which was still opening. The pilgrims threw themselves to the floor of the rocket like it was the soil of a holy land and started to pray.

"God, God, our most holy God, we come not to disturb but to look at your visage. You, the Creator and Destroyer of all, we give tribute and love and thank you as always for our continued existence." It was said in a chorus, the words prescribed. Bryan felt a twinge of guilt at not joining in, but he was going to be in the Academy now and he must put aside superstition and the old ways. He was going to be a space explorer and a modern man.

He said Blessed Be with the pilgrims and regretted not saying the whole prayer with them. Then he helped the old man up from his knees because he was still a polite boy, and he walked out into the station to start his new life.

Coming home had gotten harder over the years. Poppa was getting old, still farming, but he let Martyn drive the plow. At least that's what Momma's letters said. It had been years since he'd seen them.

He piloted himself into the landing field and touched down smoothly. He could see a large group of people on the edge of the field. He recognized Martyn, and Amy; he guessed the children standing around them were theirs. She was holding a new one he had never met; he tried to remember if it was a boy or a girl and whether he'd sent a gift. Poppa was sitting in prayer up on the cart, and Momma stood on the ground, holding a grandchild's hand. She looked smaller than even the last time he'd been home.

How long had it been? Three years, he thought to himself. It had been three years. He had given so many excuses why he couldn't be there to meet his nieces and nephews and go to the weddings of all his siblings. He'd talked to his parents every month, but he felt like he didn't belong here anymore. They were people he scarcely knew. When he'd left, he'd left as a representative of Farmtyn, but he was now no longer of Farmtyn and represented nothing they believed in.

He looked down at his watch. Tomorrow was Sunday. They would insist on dragging him along to church and showing their space explorer son off to the community. The 'ultimate pilgrim' they had called him last time, as if he was only studying star charts and looking into space as a way to see God. He breathed in and pushed it out again. The only God he prayed to now was the one he cursed under his breath when he stubbed his toe. There was no God, just space, and planets and stars and galaxies and black holes and the beauty of nebula and mathematics. They wouldn't understand.

Dinner was painful. Poppa read a verse slowly while the children stirred at the children's table but quietly because they knew better. Martyn had three children now. His second son—the baby in Amy's arms—had been named Bryan after him the same way that he had been named after his uncle. He felt a little guilty that he wouldn't be there to watch the child grow. He hoped that he would see his namesake uncle at church tomorrow. It made him remember the long line of people who had come before him. Hardworking, devout people who lived the same life as their ancestors before them despite the changes in the universe around them.

The food sat on the table, but no one would serve themselves until the prayers were finished. Poppa's voice droned on. "And so the people roamed the galaxies, and the universe was populated by man and then man in his zeal to know all and conquer all reached the edge of the universe and there he found something his science could not comprehend. He found God, the God, God of all Creation and Destruction. And in his ignorance he disturbed God, the God, the one God of Creation and Destruction. And with that God smote man and rained down upon them his ire. And man was scattered and reduced to servants of the land and the sea. And the sky was free of man so that God could rule it in peace. And so it was and so it shall be, that man should leave God in his heavens undisturbed and live in harmony with the sea and the land, and the land shall support him and his children and his children's children." Poppa looked up and directly at Bryan and Bryan could feel his unspoken anger. Bryan looked around the table at his father's children and their children's children and felt more like a stranger than he ever had. Even when he'd first arrived at the Academy, he hadn't felt this alone.

At the Academy everything had been a struggle. The other students had arrived from planets with computers and space stations. They'd learned physics and advanced science in school. He'd only been taught calculus because it helped a man fill his fishponds. The kids had snickered and called him slow as he sat struggling to finish one equation. And for a long time he was the slowest, but he didn't give up. "Slowpoke from slowest place ever. They think riding a horse is going the fast way." It was said to his face by the biggest boy in the class, a large wall of a man-child, and Bryan struggled to ignore it. He was an outsider, always having to work harder than everyone else just to keep up.

He remembered going to bed in the dormitory with a text-book on nuclear reactions and waking up with the book digging into his face. He'd forgotten to do his prayers before he slept and he'd started to pray in his bed, "God, our God, the God, the only God, forgive me my trespasses and slumber in peace. For the age of man is short and the time of God is long. Blessed Be."

He'd heard a snickering from another bed, and then a snorting laugh somewhere in the dark. "Superstitious primitive," snarled a voice. And he'd sworn to himself to never pray out loud again. Their laughter and derision had clung to him. He used it to help power himself. He was never going to be one of them so he would need to be better. He studied harder, and worked harder, and trained harder, and stopped praying at all, for that was just wasted time on his journey. He hadn't taken a vacation or time out for himself in years. And it had paid off. He had graduated first in his class.

He'd come home then to celebrate with his family. That was six years ago, but they thought he was coming home to live. Momma had lined up all the local girls to meet him at church, while Poppa had started saving seed for his son to start his own planting on his own fields, which he would need to carve like his father had before him from the wilderness that surrounded the town.

His life was already planned for him—to clear 40-50 acres, build a cabin from the trees he cleared, build a barn for the animals he would raise, and marry a girl and bring 5-10 youngsters into the world who would all do the same. And then when he was old and too tired to work anymore, give his farm to one of his children or their children and they would look after him while he slowly died.

And perhaps if life was good and he was lucky enough he would one day take a trip to the space station to look out on the stars through a telescope and make prayers to a God for peace and a long life of doing exactly what everyone before him had done. Bryan had felt the shudder go through him; his people were superstitious primitives. He had already seen more stars than anyone ever in his family. And he had flown amongst them, plotted their motions and knew their chemical compositions and the larger galaxies they lay within.

Amy had been waiting for him when he came home as a new graduate. She'd thrown herself at him, and he could see Martyn watching her as she almost choked him. He'd pushed her away towards Martyn. Then he stopped and announced before there could be any more misunderstandings that he was going to only be home for 24 hours, then he would be going back to join the Stellar Exploration Force. He hadn't known for sure he was going to go into the Force until he heard the words leave his lips. Amy had turned from him and started to weep; Martyn had gone to comfort her. Momma had turned to Poppa and Poppa had said, "As God wills it." Bryan had taken that as a sign of approval. Now, six years later, Poppa obviously disapproved of his life and his work.

"Poppa, is there something you would like to say to me?" Bryan asked, no longer the scared boy who wanted nothing more than his father's approval.

"Don't," mewed his mother.

"Let the man say his thoughts," said Martyn, more of the leader of the house now than his father was.

"Yes, please, Poppa, tell me what it is you want to say," said Bryan, sure already that he knew what it was.

"Your letter said," his father began, "that you were going on a deep space mission."

"And you don't want me to go," Bryan responded.

"Of course we don't want you to go," responded his mother, her opinions and tongue both sharper than they had been when Bryan was still a child.

"It's not that simple," said his father. "If it is God's will that you go, you will go. I am just worried."

"Of course he's worried; you could die out there," wailed his mother.

"Or wake God and kill us all," said Martyn.

The kids had gone quiet at the kids' table. Most of them weren't old enough to understand the conversation, only to understand that the older people were angry.

"Let him speak," said Bryan, wanting to have it all over, have it all said and done. "Of what do you worry, Poppa?"

"I am not sure. Of what they have said, perhaps. But even more I am afraid we have lost you."

Bryan, who knew for sure before his father spoke that he was going to be told what to do, thought he understood his father. The certain man of his youth, the firm hand that ruled the family would have forbidden him to go out on the deep space mission and he, the young boy and rebel of the family, would have yelled that he couldn't be stopped. He would have gone on the mission just to prove that he could. The same way he'd studied harder than everyone else just to prove that he wouldn't be beaten by them. He'd worked harder than everyone just to show that he, a little farm boy from Farmtyn, could not only become a space farer but a deep space explorer. He would show he wasn't afraid of the superstitions of his youth and religions of his people. That he would do the unthinkable and prove to everyone how brave he was and how wrong they all were. And in his father's reply, Bryan's certainty was shaken.

Somehow all the motivations for his life were shown in relief as the silly actions of an immature boy playing chicken. He wouldn't be the one who flinched first. And then that flicker of doubt disappeared. He was Lt. Bryan Myberry, and he had been top of his class, top cadet in the Academy. He had been places and done things his parents could not even imagine. He alone had been chosen to go on the new deep space mission. He would be fine.

"I will not get lost," Bryan responded, knowing that he was not addressing his father's concerns but wanting to have an answer to the unspoken terrors. He knew that his father was probably right. He was probably lost to them. He had moved so far from them and their teachings, and he didn't want to find his way back. Losing his religion had been a slow process. It had started when he had left and been finished by the death of his faith only a couple of years later. He no longer believed in anything the Holy Books said, and by extension he no longer believed in his father, in his people and in the future the people he loved had laid out for him. But he could tell them none of that. He felt a deep aching within knowing that he was separate from them, alone, now, and for the rest of his life.

"All right," said his father. "Let us eat." For the rest of the meal little was said as the food that was just as amazing as he remembered was consumed in abundance.

He felt guilty as he ate, that he would probably never move back home, probably never marry a good girl and raise children for his parents to hold and sing to. If he ever married or had children, his wife probably would find the idea of washing the child in front of a church a superstitious and backward idea.

At church on Sunday he had entered quietly with the family and sat in the usual seats. All eyes were on him, looking for the changes that would mark him as holy, as the ultimate pilgrim having traveled amongst the stars.

He sat only half listening to the preacher drone on about the God who should be left to slumber and about man's duty to be a servant to the earth and the sea. And he felt the sermon was directed at him and that all eyes were on him. He looked away from the preacher and down the pew to his uncle Bryan. In the few years since he'd last seen him his uncle had aged, his hair thinned and gray, his face lined by the outdoor work and the harsh sun. Uncle Bryan smiled at him, and he smiled back. He had missed his family and he knew he would continue to miss them.

The mission they were sending him on was the longest they had ever planned. He would leave the station and travel outwards for two and a half years, then turn around and head for home. It would be a long five years for him, but since he would accelerate to 90% of light speed the time dilation would mean he was gone almost twelve years. He had to wonder how his father, his uncle, even his brother would look the next time he saw them. He looked over at the two older children sitting between Martyn and Amy, in their best black going to church outfits, their shoes shined, gleaming in the colored light of the stained-glass windows, and the baby in Amy's arms. The next time he saw that baby she would be thirteen, a young woman, already a person. And that little boy who tried so hard not to fidget, the one who had been named for him, would almost be a man, ready to start clearing his own land for his own farm and his future family.

Bryan sighed. When they said he'd be gone twelve years he hadn't really thought it long but now, looking at the faces of these children, he realized it would be a lifetime.

"And listen," continued the preacher. "The words of the books are clear. God had toiled and on the edge of the forever he slept. Only slowly, imperceptibly, did he move, move in his dreams, and as he moved, he started back towards the center of existence, and once he reached the center there would be nothing. But this would take a billion millennia, unless he were woken. And he was startled—so saith the book—by the vainglory of man. For man, not content in his own realm, had reached out to the edge of the universe and there he touched God. And God was disturbed from his peaceful and pleasant dreams, and he smote man, and all of man's equipment and machinery."

Bryan looked over at the baby in Amy's arms. She would hear stories of him, her uncle Bryan, but he would be a myth, no more substantial than the God in church.

The preacher continued on, "And all the rockets stopped, and all the technology stopped, and man was left to start again, and man strove to reach the stars again. But man had been fortunate that God had not fully awoken, and sped up his journey back to the start of creation for God, our God, the God who is the God of both Creation and Destruction, and his journey outward built our reality and his journey inward will delete it from existence. So let us pray together. God, our God, the God from which all life began, rest peaceful in your slumber and dream for us the best of worlds. For the ages of man are short and the time of God is long. Blessed Be."

"Blessed Be," chanted the congregation as one. Bryan looked around at their faces, and knew he no longer belonged. They were one, with their faith and certainty, and he had nothing. He needed to leave. He needed to leave quickly.

He burst into the sunlight at the end of the service with all the speed of his youth, but he was a man now and had to slow down. He looked around at the young girls who had flirted with him when he was too young to understand that they were. They were all married now, mothers most of them, standing in their family circles. Marybel was standing over by the door. She gave him a good hard look up and down, then reached over to give her husband a kiss on the check and touched her pregnant stomach as if to tell him what he'd missed out on.

His uncle's hair shone with silver streaks in the sun as he strode towards Bryan, his long, loose legs still stomping his invisible water boots through a muddy paddock, even when he had his church shoes on. "So nephew, you dying to get out of here and back into your stars."

"Is it so obvious?"

His uncle put an arm around his shoulder and pulled him away to the edge of the crowd. Bryan was only slightly surprised they were the same height. "You were always the kid who had to climb further out on the limb than anyone." He nodded over to Martyn and Amy paying court to the preacher. "Martyn is suited to this life. He's like your Poppa. You're more like me, restless." Uncle Bryan looked out to his wife, a sweet woman, small and forgiving. "Maybe you were cursed when you were named for me."

"But you never left..."

"I never got the chance. Go, do everything you need to do to get the restlessness gone, boy. We will be here when you come back."

"It will be 12 years."

"Even if it's 30, do everything you need to do so when you come back next time you are ready to stay. We will be here, doing the same things we have always done. Farmtyn will wait and welcome you home, even when your Poppa and I are gone." Uncle Bryan patted him on his head and walked back to his wife, who smiled as he approached. His uncle may never have gotten to wander but he'd been loved.

Bryan counted the minutes till he could leave again, the way he had once counted the days till New Year's Feast. He kissed his family goodbye and left them all on the launch pad, his father and brother on their knees, praying for his safe return, while he gave a silent prayer for a quick getaway.

He had no doubts left. He was taking the mission, and when he got back to the station, he told the colonel as soon as he landed. He walked into the office with its antique wooden desk and stood at attention until he was acknowledged.

"Lt. Bryan Myberry reporting for duty, sir."

The colonel looked up from his desk. "So, Myberry, are you ready for the deep space mission?"

"Yes, sir. I have said goodbye to everyone."

The colonel looked him up and down. "You've always been determined, Myberry, but are you certain? Five years alone is hard on a man in space, and 12 years away from your people is hard for your people planet-side."

"Yes, sir. I am ready."

The colonel stood up and walked around his desk to Bryan. He held out a hand. "I believe you are." He shook his hand. "Report to Operations to begin the briefings."_____

He wrapped a blanket around his eyes to sleep. He would be passing close to a giant blue star and the light penetrated everything. He had already put a blanket against the windows, but he was having trouble sleeping. Most of the day he kept busy, just doing the experiments and tests and writing reports back to the Station. It was the nights that were long when every day was a night full of stars and every night was just a clock telling him to sleep.

He'd forgotten to sleep for three days while he passed close to the last star. Finally, he'd noticed that his head was aching in a way that pain medication couldn't fix, and he'd laid down and not awoken for sixteen hours, till the alarms in the cabin rang because he hadn't sent a message to HQ for twelve hours. He'd set an alarm after that so that he slept at least six hours in every twenty-five. It was just difficult when everything was fully lit, and he was thinking about clearing all the supplies out of the supply closet and sleeping in there. He was just worried about how much it would feel like a coffin.

He suggested to HQ in a report that future rockets be equipped with shutters and started on a project to fashion some for himself using the empty food containers as he ate through his supplies.

He sent a message to HQ every day, and he didn't know if they received them for he was out of range of their transmissions. If they did get them they would be delayed by months or longer. Traveling back through the cosmos at the speed of light, it would still take them some time to get back to the Station.

Every other day he sent a message to his Poppa and Momma. He was sure they would share them with the family, so he didn't feel the need to write Martyn or any of his other siblings. He did write a few messages directly to his Uncle Bryan, but they were filled with the thoughts and fears he couldn't send to either the colonel at HQ or his parents. Sometimes he was afraid he would go crazy, and other times, all on his own, he was sure that he already had.

"Uncle Bryan," he wrote, "I dream I am home, that I married Amy and that we had children. And then I wake alone in a metal box hurtling through space and I question all of my decisions. The stars are more beautiful seen from Farmtyn, just speckles of hope and promise. Up close they are wild, angry, terrifying beasts. Still beautiful in the way a cornered bobcat is beautiful, but unsettling and frightening. I wonder if that is what our good books talk about. Whether our ancestors flew up into the sky, got close to a star and ran back to the planet frightened, with stories of the great God of Creation and Destruction. For there is so much destruction in the light of a star—its fiery swirling gas tentacles sometimes reach out for my vessel—and yet there is also creation, for without the suns of our systems none of the life we know would exist. I know you won't pass this on to my parents. You understand that no matter what happens I am glad I am here, and even if I die out here in the darkness, please take comfort that I would always choose this life again."

Even as he wrote it, he realized it was probably a lie. A lie for his uncle to justify everything he'd done, and also lying to himself. It was two weeks before he was due to blast off that he had met Adyn, the Farmtyn ambassador. He'd come to briefing and sat in the back. It was in a bigger room than needed, a small lecture hall, and Bryan sat up front with Colonel Pierce while the scientists began the briefing. Adyn had snuck in after the lights were off, and while the head scientist, a beautiful woman Bryan wondered only briefly if she were married, began to speak.

"We are here." She pointed to a vague area towards the outside left edge of the galaxy. Bryan's awareness of the beautiful woman was replaced instantly with the awareness of her condescending attitude. He was just an astronaut. He'd spent his whole life being talked down to, so he knew the feeling well, like ice cubes down his spine. She continued, oblivious as to how disappointed he was. "The center of the galaxy is here, obviously, with the densest clusters of stars. The question is what is here." She pointed out to the edge of the galaxy to an area that in the picture was black, the edge of the galaxy. "From what we can see, the galaxy and universe as we know it end at this point. The question is why? Is this just an illusion because there are no stars? We know that the universe contains much more matter than we can possibly see, and the theory is that out here, past the stars, lies black matter.

"So we are sending you out, Mr. Myberry—" she knew his name, so at least there was that "—to see if you can take a sample of this black matter, or whatever is there. The plan is that you go out past the gravity well of Star K9918 and send a probe out from your ship. Then you measure its progress and move your ship out further if needed and keep sending the probe out. You will have two weeks to send the probe out and then you must begin your return journey with your information."

She stopped now and looked up into his eyes. Her eyes were dark blue with golden flecks. He realized he was probably supposed to say something but instead he found himself mute.

"Mr. Myberry, I do hope I haven't bored you. Do you have any questions?"

He felt like spitting out a cliché from a movie, something like "Where have you been all my life?" Instead he just shook his head. She wasn't really that cute; just another scientist snob who thought he was beneath her. He had plenty of women who had offered to give him a good sendoff, and he'd more or less told Alicia in Engineering that they would spend his last night before the mission together, but now he was wishing he was someone the blue-eyed genius would take seriously.

"I have a question," asked Ambassador Adyn in the back row.

"Yes, sir," smiled the woman Bryan wished he knew the name of. "I don't believe we have met."

"I am Ambassador Adyn Amyson of Farmtyn, and you are the scientist I have been reading about, Dr. Chapin." He did not approach but waved a hand down at her. Dr Chapin, thought Bryan. He'd just assumed Dr. Chapin was a 50-year-old man.

"Yes, Ambassador, what would you like to know?"

"The probe you are sending—is it only going to take readings or is it equipped to take a sample?"

"A very good question." She smiled at the ambassador and Bryan wished he could think of anything to say. "The probe will at first take readings and if the readings are favorable, then take a sample."

"How do we know that a sample of this so-called black matter will be safe to bring back to civilization?" The ambassador swung his arms around.

Bryan knew the answers to that one; it wasn't like he hadn't trained for this mission for months now. "The spaceship will be equipped with enough laboratory equipment to determine the true nature of the particles before I transport them back."

Ambassador Adyn looked him up and down. "Ah yes, Lt. Bryan Myberry. We have never met. It's a pleasure to finally meet you. Do you actually feel you are a good enough scientist to perform testing on the particles before you return with them? It's not like you will be able to get help; you will be outside of the range of even our best communication devices. You will be all alone."

All alone. The full impact of that had not hit him then. The idea that even sending a message home would take years to arrive. Humans are pack animals for whom isolation is torture, isolation is death. None of that he'd understood, then.

"Yes, Ambassador, but I have the protocols I need to follow. If the probe scans show that it is within safety limits, I will get a sample of the particles and will do the testing as prescribed. Those results will be sent back here and arrive at the speed of light, so approximately one and a half years later."

"I have written all the protocols myself, Ambassador," said Dr Chapin.

"Yes, Doctor, but have you given any thought that the absence of light may not be dark matter, or anything else you can possibly imagine?"

Dr. Chapin laughed. "As a scientist, sir, finding the unexpected is always in the calculations." She turned towards Bryan. "I would like to spend some time with you this week going over all the protocols personally."

Bryan nodded, suddenly happy that he would be able to spend some time with her. "Absolutely, Doctor. I will make myself available."

Time passed as time does, with slow minutes and fast weeks. He'd been gone for almost two years. The stars had begun to thin out and he was reaching the edge of the universe. He'd already gone further than any other man. If he never made it home, at least he would have set a record.

He sent his daily report. "There are no stars in front of the vessel; just an inky darkness. This is the area we were looking to explore. I do not know if this is a cloud of some kind of light-absorbing dust and whether I will pass through it and see more stars or if this is dark matter."

Dr. Chapin had explained dark matter to him in detail. By this time he was calling her Arri and she was drawing the star map with her finger down his chest and across to his navel. "Dark matter must exist. Without it nothing makes sense. There must be more mass in the universe, but we have been looking for it in all the explored regions of the galaxy and we can find no trace of it. It is possible that we just don't know how to find or measure it but there is also this big black area," she waved her arm over his legs, "and it's as good a place to look for something we can't see as anywhere."

He continued his daily report. "Star K9918 is to the starboard. At least I must assume it's K9918. It has three satellites, and they have seven moons between them. I have marked the satellites on star maps for future knowledge. They are gas giants, proto stars, and show no signs of living organisms, although this could be ascertained for certain by future expeditions. It appears to be the last system at the edge of the visible universe. The sensors show nothing in front of me, and I suspect that whatever this void consists of is unknown and therefore the computer does not register it. I know that it is not a black hole, as the computer would have easily identified one and none have ever been recorded with this type of size. It is as if the universe just ends in a blank wall of nothing."

The ambassador had invited him to dinner before he left. "May I call you Bryan?" He'd nodded, and the ambassador continued waving him into his spacious white-on-white apartment. "Please call me Adyn. I should have introduced myself earlier, but I didn't want to show favoritism."

"You were on the selection board that selected me to be a space cadet?"

"Yes, but there was a short list. Getting people to leave Farmtyn is difficult. You were the most eager; for others it would have been a punishment." The ambassador went to the bar. "Do you drink?"

"Yes." Bryan knew this wasn't a social question; it was a religious one. People from Farmtyn didn't drink or use any type of mind-altering substances. It had taken Bryan years to take his first drink and more time yet to find the joy in just letting go of himself and enjoying the moment.

"Wine or a gin and tonic?" asked the ambassador.

"Gin, please," Bryan said, sitting down and appreciating that as a space explorer, he was getting to spend time and be served by the great ambassador. He'd done some research since that day in the lecture hall. He didn't know why he'd never met the ambassador before. It would make sense that as the only two Farmtyns on the station they would be social, but they hadn't.

Bryan wondered for a moment whether the darkness in front was real, whether he had really gone to the end of the galaxy, or whether he'd just wanted to be there so much that he saw something that wasn't there. He hadn't gone as far as the computer models had indicated. He wondered if that was actually Star K9918 or one closer, whether K9918 still existed. Maybe it was already gone, fallen into the blackness, and the message of its demise just hadn't reached the station before he left. He wondered how Arri was doing. He'd sent her as much information as he could every report, samples of space analyzed and reported back. No signs of dark matter; just something to pass the time. A way to reach out to her. Every day he would send her something and she would get his messages weeks and months apart. By the time he returned she would be twelve years older. Twelve years of not sleeping in the crook of his arm. Twelve years of not waking him up by watching him with her blue laughing eyes. Twelve years... how would she look? Would she be gray when he got back, or married, or even alive? He couldn't tell.

"I am sending out a probe," he continued the report. "I believe I have reached a point where it is safest to stop my approach. It seems that I am considerably short of what was believed would be my final destination, but the protocols would indicate that now is the time for the probe to be utilized."

He'd had so much time to think about the last weeks, the last days before he left the station. In the ambassador he felt like he had met his first friend since he left home. They'd sat on the couch with their gin and tonics. "How was your last visit home?

"It was difficult," answered Bryan.

"Let me guess; your father told you not to go on this mission."

"Worse," smiled Bryan sadly. "He told me that in the end I would go if it were God's will."

Adyn laughed. "It's hard, isn't it? Stepping out beyond the people you love, losing faith?"

"Yes," Bryan said, happy there was someone else who would understand, with whom he could share his loss. Someone with whom he could mourn. "I don't belong at home anymore."

"And this is why I remain here. I keep asking for my term as ambassador to be renewed and the elders allow it. They understand that I don't belong back on Farmtyn anymore, and they don't really want to send out another person to be corrupted."

Bryan took a big gulp of his drink. "My family is still expecting me to come home."

Adyn nodded and walked back to the bar to make them more drinks. Bryan walked out to the ambassador's window with its panoramic view of distant suns and a ball of reflected light that Bryan knew was his home planet. The ambassador brought a couple of new drinks to Bryan at the window. "They say that you will be the last cadet. They say that this deep space mission is the final sacrilege. Until now there has been one cadet every 20 years, and now they say they can no longer support the program. Superstitious bastards! They know their little cult can't stand up in the way of science. They don't want Farmtyn to ever progress. They are even going to stop teaching any type of science or advanced math."

"I am the last?"

"Yes. Cheers," said Adyn and threw back the drink.

There was a loneliness in the knowledge that he would be the last of his people to explore the stars. Adyn understood this loneliness and in him he found a friend. For they had lost their faith and with it their connection to their people, to their planet, to their home. And for the next few weeks, while Bryan trained for the mission, they would meet and enjoy a meal and a drink. They both knew they would never find their faith again, that it was gone forever. And Bryan tried to fill the void with Adyn and Arri and witty evenings in his suite of rooms, the three of them enjoying drinks and laughing about the irony of the slowest, most backward planet in the universe providing the astronaut that would soon fly further and faster than anyone ever had.

"They are threatening to shut off the planet," yelled Adyn in the hallway, catching him on his way to yet another simulation practice.

"What do you mean?"

"They say if we don't cancel this mission they will cut off all ties to the Federation and close down all space travel."

"But the pilgrims?" said Bryan.

"Not just that; all of the grain and food that is imported to this station. The station will starve. I have talked to the elders, and they have agreed to maintain the exports of food stuffs as letting it rot would be wasteful, but they are no longer permitting the people of Farmtyn to leave the planet. The Space Commission doesn't understand. They told me to tell them that they are cutting their people off from space travel and expansion onto other planets. The elders of Farmtyn say they have already had space travel and that their people are already throughout the galaxy. They told the Space Commission that their planet was enough for 20 more generations and that by then God would return and life would begin again."

"Oh wow. I am so sorry, Adyn. And you are stuck in the middle of this. What are you going to do?"

"The Commission is going to send your mission despite their threats, and your mission will prove that space travel is safe. So, I guess for the next few years I placate Farmtyn enough to keep the station fed."

It was time for the next protocol. He stopped the vessel then pushed the button to launch the probe, and watched the screen as it moved away from him. It had a light for visual inspection, but the darkness was not illuminated. The probe moved out from him for two days, recording nothing. No mass, no wavelengths, not even changes in gravity.

There was just nothing there.

Bryan thought about Arri and about the curve of her shoulder. That little hollow he could make her giggle just by kissing. This was not the information she wanted. She wanted there to be something, something solid or measurable at least.

The clock on his dashboard said the probe had enough fuel for 4 more days, then he would need to retrieve it. When it returned he could advance his ship to the probe's farthest point, refuel it, and send it out again. That was the protocol. He could do that four times before he would need to return empty handed.

How would Arri take the news that he had found nothing, that the entire trip had been in vain? Twelve years waiting for information, and he would have nothing to give her. He wanted so much to be able to give her a sample of her black matter, something to make all her work worthwhile.

The probe kept going. He could see it visually, a little dot of white like a firefly flying out against a sky not so much black as devoid of light. The cameras on the probe sent him back imagery, black images of blackness without even so much as the reflection of the light from the probe bouncing off minute particles. This part of space was a void without even space dust.

Then the probe stopped—a little dangling ball of light in the distance—like it had hit a wall. Bryan checked all the gages.

They registered nothing. He checked the probe's readings. The probe was still functional, the motor that had propelled it through space was still at maximum speed. Only the probe had stopped.

He checked all the sensors again. There were no readings. No tractor beam holding it still. No energy readings of any kind. No mass readings. No gravity. The readings were the same as they had been for days now, but the probe was no longer moving; it was suspended in space.

Bryan turned on all the sensors to full sensitivity, even the audio. And he thought he could hear something, like a gentle breathing, a slow, rhythmic vibration.

He projected the image from the probe's camera onto the full screen. Nothing; just darkness. He moved the camera angle—darkness, more darkness. Then something illuminated from the light on the probe showed on the screen for a second.

"No, it cannot be!" he screamed, and the probe disappeared.

He threw himself to his knees and began to pray, "God, our God, the God, the only God, forgive me my trespasses and slumber in peace. For the age of man is short and the time of God is long. Blessed Be. God, our God, the God, the only God, forgive me my trespasses and slumber in peace. For the age of man is short and the time of God is long. Blessed Be. God, our God, the God, the only God, forgive me my trespasses and slumber in peace. For the age of man is short and the time of God is long. Blessed Be...."

Chapter Two

Steve the Sloth

S teve walked up to the automatic door and it swung slowly open. "Hello and have a peaceful day." He wished it would open faster. As soon as he could he walked into the building, sliding past the people dawdling in front of the elevator or meandering in the lobby, and made his way to the stairs; no one would slow him down on the stairwell.

"Good morning, Steve. Why, aren't you in a hurry this morning! Would you like to stop and get a coffee before you go into the office?" It was Larry, his supervisor, sitting on the sofa in the lobby, coffee in hand, looking up from a plate full of beignets, his face covered in powdered sugar he hadn't dusted off.

"No, Larry. I have a lot to do."

"What could be more important than a good breakfast, Steve?" Larry waived a beignet at him then dunked it in his coffee and slurped it up. Steve kept moving before Larry could open his full mouth and keep talking.

Steve walked into the office, the first one in as usual, and turned on his computer. Emails; he looked to see what was being reported. There would be no work tomorrow because of power reductions. He groaned. Not again. He didn't really like being at home. There wasn't enough to do to keep him busy. At work he did his own job, video editing for television, and at the same time worked on his own project—a video-editing software program that could slow down and speed up film. He knew it would make his life so much easier. He was tired of looking at film for hours on end cutting and splicing.

He read the rest of the emails. The boss told him that the show he was working on was renewed for another 10 or so episodes. So, he had at least a year of work ahead of him on that show, and they wanted to hire another four video editors for the other three shows they had coming online. Steve wanted to scream at them for that. He could do it all, but they wouldn't believe him. He fired up the news. Another 200 people had been killed when traffic lights failed to work in the central city and a bus (which was just out of the repair shop) did not have brakes. That brought the deaths by accident in the city to 1202 for the year.

He wrote down 1202 on a piece of notepaper and taped it to his monitor, replacing the note from yesterday which said 987. It was only February. He felt like he was the only one that noticed or cared. He put the pen down and went to get a coffee.

Everyone was slowly arriving into the office and he made sure he made enough for everyone. No one had cleaned out the machine the night before and the coffee shot through bitter and black, but Steve didn't know it could be any other way. He washed out a paper cup—since no one had ordered new ones—and breathed in the smell with pleasure.

He picked up this camera and set it up on his desk pointing out towards the people ambling in. He hit record. He needed some video to work with on his computer software. What could be better than people arriving? Arriving, heading towards the kitchen to get coffee. He could see the pleasure on their faces as they poured coffee into their own dirty paper cups. They did the same thing every morning and yet not one thought to ask who had prepared the coffee for them so it would be ready when they entered.

He grabbed his coffee cup, added some cream and stirred it with a stick. He turned to get some sugar packets, tore one and poured it in. But the stir stick was gone. He fished his finger into the coffee looking for the stick but it wasn't there. He could have sworn he'd already stirred the coffee. It looked like he had; the color was nicely uniform. He turned to grab another stir stick and as he went to put it into his coffee, he saw there was already one there.

He shook his head, tore open a sugar packet and stirred it with the stir stick, but the stick was gone. That was it. He was really losing his mind. There was no other answer to it. Of course there hadn't been a stick in the drink already. It must have just been a trick of the light.

He grabbed his drink and went to his desk. The note had fallen, and he picked it up, sticking it back up. 1202. He knew he couldn't do anything about it, but it seemed like he was the only one even noticing and he didn't want to forget. 1202 people were dead just because no one cared about anything anymore. Everyone was just concerned about taking it easy, enjoying their lives, their days, as if their lives and their days were the only ones that mattered. Steve felt that taking it slow, not stressing, hadn't always been the way of the world. If it had been, he reasoned, then humanity would have died out years before.

He was deep in his work and had finally worked out how to speed and slow down film when the majority of his work mates showed up. It had taken him a year to work out how to digitize the film and then the software to manipulate it, but he had it. He would be able to do his job in a fraction of the time. No more looking at the film, cutting it with a knife and gluing it to the next piece; he'd be able to cut everything together on the computer. He blessed the man who had invented the computer only a century before. Now he could use it for his job, not just email and cat videos. He pushed the film from yesterday's shoot into the machine and started editing. He was finished with it by the time most of the office had filed in and out of the breakroom with the coffee he had made.

Now he was bored. He looked at the number on the note. 1202. On a whim, he went to the footage taken from the crash and sent it into his digitizer. Then he added the footage from yesterday's ferry sinking, then back and back he went, looking for the footage from all the news reels. Suddenly he realized everything was quiet. Everyone had left and he was all alone in the office.

He hadn't eaten or drunk anything since that first coffee. It was time to go home. He reached over to take a mouthful of the cold coffee and found it surprisingly warm and pleasant. He didn't remember refilling it, but he must have. He picked up his coat and headed home for the night. To another night alone with his cat and the television showing the disasters about him.

He was back in the office before anyone else the next day, making the coffee as usual. When he sat down at the computer to finish his digitization of disaster footage he found more in footage in the file than he'd remembered scanning in. Maybe Larry was right, maybe he was working too hard.

The new software made his job so much easier. He was watching the latest video of a bus crash. They wanted the footage on the news tonight and someone had captured it on their phone. An old man was crossing the road as the bus approached. He was drunk and stumbling head-forward, oblivious to his own location, trying to get home to lie down face-first possibly in his own vomit. His gray hair was blowing in the wind when the bus turned the corner. The bus driver saw the old man and swerved right, but the wheel fell off the bus. The bus jolted to the left and fell on its side. It was skidding towards the old man. There was no way they weren't going to hit him. There was no way to save him.

Steve grimaced knowing what was to follow, but didn't shut his eyes, just squinting at the screen like one would at the sun, as if it would lessen the impact. The bus ran up to the old man and the old man flew. He flew forward without even looking around to see the bus. He leapt up and fell sprawled just a few inches past the wheels of the bus. Then the old man got up, shook his head and kept walking, while behind him the surviving passengers climbed out of the bus windows and onto the street.

Steve shook his head and opened his eyes. It wasn't possible. He rewound the film and watched it again. Watching it the third time, he suspected the old man was so drunk he never even knew the bus had crashed behind him. He showed no sign of seeing it or observing anything. So how had an old man, too drunk to notice a hurtling bus even after it had crashed, leapt into the air to avoid being hit by it? Steve rewound it again and this time sped down the film. The old man was barely moving. The bus was coming. The old man was directly in its path. And then a blur. Steve stopped the film and looked. A ghost was moving across the road, a shadowy figure out of focus. Steve moved the film forward as slowly as possible. The ghost moved towards the old man. Then stopped. Now that it stood still he could tell it was definitely a figure of a man, not a reflection or trick of the light. The ghost bent down and lifted the old man, throwing him into the air, then moved as a blur out of frame.

Steve watched it again.

And again.

He thought about showing it to Larry, or Mr. Howard, Larry's supervisor. He stood up and looked to the big bosses' office. Mr. Howard and Larry were standing in Mr. Howard's room. They were throwing darts at a picture of the president. Steve shook his head and rewound the film again.

He grabbed his coffee. But the cup was empty. He put it back down and rewound it again. He wished the quality of the film were better. But it was a man. In blue pants and a white shirt, with brown hair. He was a big man; not huge but full-sized. Steve grabbed for his coffee cup again, forgetting it was empty.

He swallowed a big gulp of hot coffee, almost choking on how hot it was. He didn't remember filling it up. He must be losing his mind.

He went to grab his pen and write down the time stamp of the mystery man, but it was gone again, probably rolled off the desk. Steve dug around and found another pen and wrote it down. He made the normal speed copy for the news desk that evening. At normal speed the man was completely invisible.

Steve took the next piece of film and put it in the machine. And then he slowed the film down. As far down as possible. And as the commuter train derailed he saw the streak again, and another streak, and children were pulled back to safety. The streaks moved quickly, appearing besides bystanders and pushing them quickly backward out of danger.

By the time he'd seen them at 4 different disasters, he had a theory. The toddler who jumped out of the burning building safely was both thrown and caught. The girl who fell out of the building when the window fell out was caught, then shielded from the falling glass.

Steve realized he'd been sitting too long. He had gone numb and his legs were falling asleep. He looked around and realized that he was alone in the office again. He looked down at this coffee cup and wondered if he truly was alone. Maybe everyone had a guardian angel with them at all times. He wasn't sure what else it could be. He wrote down his theory on a postage note and put it on his monitor. Guardian Angels?

He took the film he had taken of the office, of people arriving and leaving, and started to digitize it. Would there be angels in the office? Would everyone come in with their own angel? His stomach started to growl and he realized he couldn't keep going. It was far too late. He went to rinse out his cup and go home, too tired to keep his eyes open anymore.

He came in to work late the next morning. He'd tossed and turned all night, unable to sleep but too tired to be awake. He walked into a log jam of people crowded around the break room. They were standing there with coffee cups in hand, confused and dismayed.

Margaret, the receptionist who was always watching soap operas at her desk, was not only missing her soap operas but apparently also not manning the phone at all. "Steve, do you know how to get the coffee machine going again? It always has coffee, only today it didn't."

Steve stared at her. This was what was wrong with society. Everyone just assumed everything worked and no one needed to do anything in particular to make it work. There was no effort, no follow through. It was a wonder anything got done at all. Steve was sure it hadn't always been this way. After all, the buildings they came to work in had been there hundreds of years, cars that were made eighty years before were still driving the streets, even the coffee machine was probably a hundred years old. What had happened? Was he the only one trying to make anything better, to do something new? Was he the only one who cared?

He pushed everyone aside and snarled at them, "Go back to your desks. I will make the coffee. It will take ten minutes. Leave me alone until it's done."

Everyone except Jo in HR scurried off. "Do you mind if I watch how it's done?" she asked. "So I can do it too?"

He turned back to look at her. Perhaps this was how humanity survived, on the back of a few people who did more than the minimum necessary. The one in a hundred who tried something new, tried to help. He smiled at her, sorry she had been one of the ones he's snarled at. He'd never really spoken to her before. He knew who she was. He'd picked his paycheck up from there enough times. He looked at her with new appreciation and showed her how to put the coffee in and start the machine.

"Would you like to go to lunch with me?" he asked, instantly regretting he'd said anything.

She smiled.

She was probably married, or in a relationship, or thought he was ugly or just an asshole for snapping.

"Yes, sure—how about tomorrow?"

He found himself smiling, his lips pulling back from his teeth in a way both unaccustomed and uncomfortable. "Yeah, sure, great. 12?"

"Sure" she smiled back. "I'll meet you at your desk."

He walked back to his desk and instantly saw the Post-It notes—"1202," "Guardian Angels"—and he was sorry he'd spoken to her. He had work to do. When she came at noon tomorrow he would just tell her he couldn't go. Picking up from the night before, he went to the film that he had been digitizing but it was gone. He dug through his desk and it wasn't there. He went to look at the digital copy and it wasn't saved. There was no record of what he had done last night. What had happened? Had he forgotten to save it? Had the cleaning people accidentally thrown out the film? He looked around. The cleaning people hadn't even emptied the waste paper baskets; how could they have thrown out his film? He rewatched the bus video as slowly as possible. It was impossible, but there it was. He leaned forward and then he saw the message. It had been typed and added into the film.

He could have missed it. It blinked so fast. He tried to rewind and see it again.

Words, yes, but so fast he could barely see them, like he could barely see the angel in the video saving the man. So very fast. He practiced now, practiced clicking at precisely the right moment so he could freeze the screen.

There it was, frozen, slightly shaking. "Hi, Steve. We are not angels. Stop pursuing this now. Or you will disappear."

Steve looked around. He wanted confirmation. He wanted to know he wasn't losing his mind. He went to Jo's desk. "Look, I'm sorry to disturb you. There's something on my screen. Could you come take a look?"

She smiled up at him. "Sure. Vivian, my boss, already said I should take an early lunch and go home." She smiled at him with the kind of smile that said Vivian had probably added something about him and getting lucky but she was too much of a lady to mention it.

Jo walked swiftly back to his desk, keeping up with him as he almost ran back. The screen was black when they got to his desk. Black like the computer had died. "Oh that," said Jo, looking at the black screen. "My computer did that last year, and it was the hard drive. I lost all my files."

"Oh no, no, no..."

"It's ok, Steve, I'll see what I can do," she said, jumping in and pushing several keys and rebooting the system. The screen slowly started to reopen. "Wow, looks like you are in luck." She typed quickly and accurately, pulling up his hard drive. "You haven't lost much; just the files from the last week or so."

"Damn."

"I'll call Tech Support." She took his phone and quickly dialed. "Hi, George. It's Jo. I am well. How about you and your family? Great. We have a problem in cubicle 124. Can you come on up? Oh, thank you, darling. That would be awesome. Yes, the system crashed and it looks like we've lost about a week of files. Thanks so much. I will leave it on for you."

She stood up and looked him in the eyes. "There is nothing you can do right now to change it. You owe me a lunch and I skipped breakfast so I'm hungry."

Steve couldn't think of an excuse fast enough to counter her motion. So he reached down, grabbed his coat and also the note that said Guardian Angels. No one repairing his computer needed to see that. He was obviously losing his mind and the fewer people knew about it the more chance he had to continue his life outside of an asylum.

They went up to the counter and ordered. "I would like a tuna sandwich," said Steve.

"There is no tuna," said the apathetic girl behind the counter while looking at the floor.

"Roast beef?"

"No roast beef." Her phone buzzed and she pulled it out of her pocket, then turned the camera on and checked her eyebrows.

"Turkey?" asked Jo.

The girl squeezed a small, blocked pore at the tip of her nose, popping out a white head while looking at her phone, and shook her head.

"Do you want to tell us what you do have?" asked Steve, his anger rising. Jo placed a hand on his arm, and he felt himself calm a little.

"Please," asked Jo.

"Chicken," said the girl examining the white lump from her nose on the back of her fingernail.

"Ok, two of those, please," said Jo and took Steve by the hand, walking him over to a table by the window.

"I hate going out to eat," said Steve. "They never have half the things on the menu."

"My grandma told me that when she was a girl people used to care. Then, well... they just didn't anymore. It was like there was no one setting an example of how to care. Everyone was just trying to be happy, and everyone forgot that it was the byproduct of a job well done, not the goal. Anyway, that's what my grandmother said." Jo blushed slightly at having given a speech.

"I like the sound of your grandmother," said Steve, looking over her shoulder at the kitchen crew who were standing around thinking about possibly making a sandwich.

"She raised me," said Jo. She looked at him intently. "I think my grandma would like you."

Steve wondered if he had lost his program. He didn't have a backup. All his work, all his effort. All the proof of the angels gone. He looked up and saw Jo looking at him. Looking at him in a way that made him wonder if she liked him. She was quite beautiful up close, with a sprinkling of freckles he hadn't noticed before. The conversation had stopped so he said, "I will go get the drinks." And stood up to break the awkward silence. He grabbed two slightly warm sodas from the fridge and handed over the money. No need to ask Jo what kind of drink she wanted; this was all they had in stock.

He sat back down, opened his soda and took a sip. It would have been better cold. He wondered what it would have been like to live in the good old days. When people cared.

"Thanks, Steve. It's so nice to meet someone who is willing to make an effort." She smiled.

He smiled back. "I am sorry I'm not better company. I made a program to slow down and speed up film and it showed me something. And, well, I am afraid I lost it."

Jo blanched. "Slow down film. So, you can see things that are moving very quickly?"

"Yes. I suppose I will have to remember the program and write it again."

"Don't do that," she barked.

"Why not?" he said.

She grabbed up her soda and headed for the door. "Come, let's see if your program has been lost."

"But our sandwiches?" He motioned at the slow-moving boys still staring at their phones in the kitchen.

"Screw the sandwiches. They will take forever. This is important. Come on."

He followed her, for the first time in his life having to move fast to keep up with another person. She picked her phone out of her pocket and speed-dialed the office. She stopped to talk, and Steve caught up. "Hi, George. Did you get to the computer in cubicle number 124 yet? Oh, you did, darling; aren't you a doll. So, what do you think? Oh, the hard drive has melted? Looks like it spun too fast and just caught fire. Oh, that's such a shame. Thank you, darling. I do very much appreciate you and how quickly you responded. Could you please order a new computer for the cubicle? Thanks, love."

She turned to Steve. "Yep, you must have done it, because your computer is destroyed. When I opened your computer it was only missing files; now it's on fire. Come on. My car's this way. I think we need to visit my grandma."

Steve followed her, confused, but she seemed so certain. He found her squared shoulders and her forward march so very attractive. Her car was obvious when he saw it. It was clean, shining in the sun. It was black. He'd never seen a black car clean before. It had been parallel-parked well against the curb while the others were parked helter-skelter. She hit the button to unlock it and climbed in. He followed her and she pulled out carefully, then drove competently and carefully on the sidewalk to get around the cars that blocked their path. He looked around the car. It was not only clean but spotless, and smelled good. He looked at her again. She was a strange girl.

They arrived at a neat-looking house with a mown lawn and flowers growing in the garden, not just weeds. Her grandma was expecting them. Jo had called her and told her all about Steve's program and computer problem on the way there. Steve didn't quite understand why; maybe Grandma was a computer expert who could fix a melted hard drive, although it seemed impossible. He followed her out of the car to the door of the house. "Hi, Grandma," called Jo, and they walked into the living room where Grandma stood by a wall of computer screens. So maybe she was a computer expert.

"Take a seat over there, Steve," said Grandma as if she knew him and pointed to a couch. She was younger than Steve had expected, and graceful and quick in her movements. She had already laid out a pot of tea, sandwiches and cookies. "Help yourself. I don't think you've had lunch yet."

Steve grabbed a plate and added a couple of sandwiches. They looked divine—tuna salad and roast beef and cheese. He poured out a cup of tea. Jo sat next to him and also filled her plate.

Jo bit into the sandwich and moaned. "Oh, Grandma, such a great lunch! Much better than I was planning on."

"Yes, of course, dear," answered her grandmother and sat across from them. "Steve, I am going to come straight to the point. Jo says you invented software that slows down film. They wouldn't have destroyed your computer if you hadn't seen them. So, tell me about the shadows on your film, the ones at the disaster scenes."

"The guardian angels? How do you know about the guardian angels?"

"Angels; I like that. Better than ghosts. What did you see?"

Steve swallowed down the sandwich and almost choked, then sucked down hot tea, scalding his mouth. He started to cough. Jo patted him on the back.

"You can tell me what you saw, Steve. I will believe you," continued Grandma.

"I saw people being saved by shadows that flew in and out across the screen. People just moved out of the way of busses, and babies were caught by angel arms, then placed on the ground as they fell out of windows and... And I know they are there, and it must be happening all over. I mean, over 1200 people in the city have died this year because of just stupid accidents but I know it would be much higher, because obviously someone or something is saving some of them, and

I don't know what it is but it's a force for good, and if I can slow film down to almost a stop I can almost see them, shaped like men but blurred and almost invisible."

"Would you like to know what you saw, Steve?"

"Yes, more than anything, but how do you—"

"I can answer your questions, Steve. Just let me tell the story first. Jo could have filled you in, but she prefers that I do it. Have you heard the children stories about fairies and fae people?" He nodded, and she continued, "In the stories they were sometimes good and sometimes evil. They could help you find lost items or just take things from you. You'd put your pen down and it would be gone. They would just take it. The stories go back into history for as long as man has told stories. There are stories of the elves, the borrowers, the pixies, brownies, kelpie, peri, imp. All the same things you see, all invisible but powerful. And then there is the story of the modern age, where no one believes in anything, and no one cares about anything. People are killed every day just because of a general malaise. It started hundreds of years ago. Man built all the things he thought he needed, and he took pills to relieve the boredom and the depression of a life too easy and too simple. The goal became being happy, not achieving anything. People wanted to be interesting, not interested in anything, and society fell apart. It started to decay slowly, with education, then the infrastructure the world depended on slowly falling apart while people took drugs and looked for ways to be happy.

"It was about 200 years ago that the last group of great scientists tried to fix the world's woes. They thought if they could send people into the past they could repair the problems of the past and correct the current woes. They turned themselves—to use your word—into angels and sent themselves back into the past to try to fix the problems that came before."

"I don't understand," Steve said, grabbing another of what were the greatest sandwiches of his life. "If they went into the past, why are they here? And why can't we see them and—"

"She likes to take her time to get to the point," said Jo and passed him a plate with cookies on it. "Try these. You will love them."

"Jo thinks you care about people. Do you, Steve? Do you care what happens to them?"

"Yes, I do—don't know why."

"Because you are supposed to. We are all supposed to. I will continue. The scientists made the machine to move them in time, but they made one mistake. By stepping out of their own timestream, they started to live in super-accelerated time. The scientists that went into the past became things of legend but traveled so quickly through the past times they were not able to effect meaningful change. They were too fast to be seen, too fast to interact in any meaningful way with the people they left behind. They decided to put their efforts into saving as many people as they could and effecting the change that was possible. They also resolved that no one should know they existed."

"So when Jo said that I must have done it because my computer was destroyed, she meant I had exposed their secret?" he asked now, wondering how many cookies he could eat. He'd never wanted to eat anything before. Everything he bought from the store was always so very boring. These cookies were different than anything he had ever had.

What Grandma was saying made sense—the pens missing off his desk, the coffee appearing in his mug. If someone could move more quickly than anyone else, they could easily do this. But why? It drew attention to them. "I just don't understand... If they are real, and they don't want anyone to know, and they destroy the evidence—why do you know? And why have they hinted to their existence? I mean disappearing pens and things."

"I thought they had started bothering you," said Jo. "See, Grandma, I told you."

"Yes, dear, and the fact that he's cute too doesn't hurt, does it?"

Jo blushed red and Steve looked at her. She thought he was cute, did she? He smiled and thought that the next time he asked her out he would like to make her blush again.

"Good questions, young man. The fact that they have been making themselves known to you means they wanted you to know that they existed. They did not, however, want you to have proof. And the reason why I know they exist is quite simple, really. I work for them."

Steve stopped chewing and contemplated the cookie in his hand. "Ok, so this is crazy."

"Jo, love, can you put your plate down on the table?" Jo put down her plate. It vanished and appeared on the floor across the room. Grandma was still sitting in her chair.

"I am not a magician, my boy, and they aren't magical or supernatural. Not demons, or fairies, or angels. They are just very, very fast." And as she said that, the plate reappeared in Jo's hand with one of the cookies gone.

"Why would they need an employee?" asked Steve.

"They needed someone on this side. And I was the obvious choice because my father was one of the original scientists. They are trying to fix this world, or at least make it less terrible. So they keep sending agents back in time to try to fix the past.

"They started by sending people to the 1960s, since they thought that was when the problems started, but nothing they did there fixed anything. So the next group were sent back to the 1950s. Those that fail to change things in the past pass through the ages to our time and try to mitigate the damage. But once they have stepped outside of our timestream they can never rejoin it. They will always move too fast for us to be able to interact in any meaningful way. I will never have another conversation with my father. But I can write him a message and he can write me a reply. And there are limitations. They can only send a person back once. If they try to send them back twice, they are so far removed from our timeline and sphere of existence that we don't know if they are dead or alive."

Steve held onto his cookie tighter, somehow wanting to protect this thing that felt like reality. "Why are you telling me all this?"

"Because Jo and I think you are a good candidate. We recruit for what you call 'the angels.' They need more people to help them. We are sending people further and further back in history to try to fix the damage. You want to help people. You are aware of what is going on around you, and you were smart enough to figure out the angels' existence already.

"So you recruit people to disappear forever?" Steve thought that should be terrifying but it wasn't.

"Yes. That's why we only recruit people who have no family, no children, no loved ones who will miss them. You won't be alone. You will be part of the greater organization—but you won't be able to come home again."

Steve thought about the note on his computer. 1202. 1202 people dead. He felt the weight of that and his own irritation with the world around him. Here was a way to do something. But then he felt something else, something he'd never experienced before.

He turned, suddenly knowing that there was a question he needed to ask. A question that could change his life. Something he needed to know the answer to before he went any further. "If I left, Jo, do you think you might miss me?"

Lust:

Chapter Three

Sex Tourist

Daniella took off her clothes and slipped on the robe, stepping into the empty waiting room and pulling the robe tight around herself as she sat down, tugging the fabric down with one hand while holding the seams together across her breasts with the other.

A long-faced bleached blonde past her prime came out of a different changing room and sat down next her. The blonde fidgeted with her nails and checked out her chipped pedicure, then turned to look at Daniella. "Hey, I'm Christina. This your first time?"

"Yes."

"It's my sixth. It'd be more but I need to make the money. This time I'm going for a week."

"That's nice."

"Yeah. I mean the one-day trips are good, don't get me wrong, but you know, a week... well, that gives you the chance to really settle in, try some new things, really experience things."

"Yes."

"I heard they experimented with one-month trips but people fell in love and wanted to stay, so they banned anything longer than a week. I mean, you know, a week is fun every month or two. It's all I can take anyway. A month... I probably wouldn't want to come back. So, when are you going?"

"Not sure."

"I went to Ancient Rome last time; it was great. But this time I'm going to try Shakespearean London. They've got a tavern wench packet with enough money to see a play. Sounds like the ticket for me. A little culture, a little alcohol, a little fucking."

Daniella winced slightly and crossed her legs, wondering if she'd made a mistake.

"I had a friend," continued Christina, "who tried the Plains Indian experience, always been crazy about boys in warpaint, but she said it was too much work and not enough play. I mean, if you go so far back, there just aren't a lot of conveniences, and it's too much culture shock. I mean, I just don't want to poo in the woods, but another friend of mine signed up for the Old Testament tour and she loved it. She told me I should totally check it out, that being a handmaiden was pretty good and there was an awful lot of begetting."

Daniella shivered again and realized she'd come to the wrong place. She was too lonely. There was no way she could enjoy this. She shouldn't have let her sister-in-law talk her into it.

"Miss Daniella, come this way." A large apple of a woman reached her hand to help Daniella out of the chair. Then she opened the door for Daniella and Daniella was coaxed out into the hallway, then down the hallway and into the transport room. Daniella wanted to flee. She looked behind her to see how she might be able to but it was impossible to squeeze past this round nurse without hitting either the wall or her gargantuan rear end. So Daniella just kept going forward until she was in the transport room, certain now that she did not want to go anywhere. She just wanted to go home. Home, where she used to live with Michael; home, where the pillow on his side still smelled like him; home, where she could still sometimes pretend he would be returning.

The transport room was white. The technicians were all in white coats too, as if that made them more official, more legitimate, not just vendors of vacations into debauchery. The room was white too and sterile, with a clear transportation pod. It looked like a glass coffin, open to inspection by all, yet comfortable and enclosed. Not like the coffin she'd put Michael in, all closed and sealed off in the darkness after the disease so no one could see how it had eaten him alive. So she couldn't see the scars from the many operations; just remember them and imagine how he looked lying there in the darkness.

"So, do you know where you'd like to go? What time period?"

"No." She was starting to shake. "I don't know."

"We can offer you any time, you know. It has been proven that the past is unchangeable, so you can travel back to any time period you would like, be your grandmother's friend, go back further to the Neanderthals, even be a man if that interests you."

"I don't think I should be here."

"Haven't you ever wanted to just go and see Shakespeare perform one of his own plays or watch Julius Cesar ride back into Rome with Cleopatra? Or you could just go meet your own mother. This trip can be what you make of it, Daniella. Can I call you Daniella? You just need to travel back to the body of someone who was an ancestor. Not a close ancestor—that is forbidden—but a distant DNA relative. We've found that causes the least disturbance to the host."

She looked around and thought of Michael. He was the only man she'd ever wanted. They were going to travel through time together. They were going to do a lot of things when he retired. He'd laughed that they'd both be young again in host bodies, frolicking across the ice at the frost fairs of London, and traveling across America naked in a luxury carriage on a steam-powered train. He'd researched all the times their DNA relatives had met. Yet none of those people were them, none of them were her alone. She didn't want to be alone.

"Of course, you can only stay a week. Longer than that and it's dangerous for the host. We may lose them altogether and you would be stuck back there. So, wherever we send you we send you with a tracker, and when it beeps you have 24 hours to get back to the place you arrived and you will return. And don't think that you don't have to return. Failure to report in is a crime."

"Yes." The walls were starting to shake and sway. Or was that her? Was she going to faint? She wanted to sit down. She wanted to go home. Home to that little house they'd bought together only 25 years ago. She'd just paid it off, made the last payments with the life insurance money. He'd be happy about that; she could stay in that house for the rest of her life.

The rest of her life. How long did she even want that to be? Why was she even here? How had she let Amanda push her into this? What was it Amanda had said, "The quickest way over one man is under another." But then Amanda had never really been in love with anyone other than herself.

"Please sit down, Miss," said the technician. "And we can bring out the catalogue if you need a couple more minutes to read the selections."

She shook her head. She didn't need to know that she could come back as a Vestal Virgin. She didn't want to be anyone else. She wanted to be herself, herself when she was happy, herself when she had Michael. "Can I come back as myself?" she asked.

"Yourself?" asked the technician, confused.

"Yes, myself—only younger; 28 years ago, to be exact."

"Well, that's most unusual. I can check." He tapped his ear and walked to the wall to speak quietly and explain the situation.

Yes, she thought. This is what I want. I know why I am here now. I don't want to be anyone else. Just me. I want to be me.

"Miss Daniella. They say it is possible, but that you must sign more waivers."

"More waivers?"

"Apparently it is more dangerous."

"How is it more dangerous? You've already told me that the past is immutable. I can't change anything that's happened. You've proven that. What's meant to be will be. I've heard it enough times, so what is dangerous about it?"

He tapped his ear again. "Bring in waiver forms J18-Z3. Thank you." He turned to her. "We have an office you can go into and sign the necessary waivers. The papers will explain everything."

She read through all the papers. So here was the reason why people didn't travel into their own pasts. Made sense if she'd thought about it. *Traveling back in time does not mean that you can control or change past events. Past events are fixed. You, the Traveler, are merely a spectator to the events that have already occurred. You may inhabit the body of someone but you may not change their actions or emotions in any appreciable way. You will experience the sensations of their body, but you are unable to influence their mind.*

This, however, changes if you go back in time to yourself in your own timeline. Visiting your own timeline, you are still just a spectator. The problems arise because the events and actions you revisit may not correspond with your own memories of them. This cognitive dissonance can, and has been shown to, destabilize the mind of the Traveler. This can lead to permanent psychosis, with the returning traveler unable to disentangle their thoughts and emotions from the thoughts and emotions both real and remembered of the former timeline. This is why we do not encourage people to reexperience their own timelines.

Daniella looked at the paperwork. It was obviously a bad idea. Everything she had read reaffirmed that it was. And now that she had realized it was possible she couldn't get the idea out of her head. She had to go back. She had to see Michael. She thought about all the times she could see him, and she knew what she wanted. She wanted to see him the way he'd been right after they got married. They'd had nothing but each other. They'd slept on that horrible futon bed in a studio apartment empty of furniture. That's when she wanted to go back, to feel his arms around her on that lumpy futon, the metal frame squeaking as they made love all night every night.

She walked back out to the waiting technician. She looked at him properly. He was almost her age. There was a name tag on the white coat and she read it out as she greeted him. "I have read the paperwork, Michael." He had the same name as her hubby, as her love. It was a sign. "I need to go back twenty eight years. To my own life."

"Ok," Michael the technician said. "The rules state that before you can tour your own life you must first take a tour elsewhere."

"But I don't want to go anywhere else."

"Tough, lady; them's the rules. You want to go—pick somewhere." It was the female technician in a voice that sounded like pure Brooklyn.

"I... I... I don't know," she stammered, ashamed at the thought of going somewhere else and traveling into someone else's life.

"Please," Michael the technician said, "take a day, take the paperwork, and come back tomorrow if you want to do this. Remember, we can only send you on one trip at a time. The minimum is two days, twenty-four hours for each. And you must pay for all travels. So this will cost at least twice as much."

"Ok," nodded Daniella and started to walk back to the cubicle to find her clothes. She had a lot to think about. As soon as she hit the train she called Amanda.

"Slow down," Amanda said. "You're talking so fast. I will meet you at your place. Let's talk then."

She got off the train and headed up to her apartment. Amanda was already there. "So what happened? I sent you to go on a vacation and get laid. What are you doing back here?"

"I asked to go back twenty-eight years."

"Twenty-eight years? That isn't fun. There was nothing fun twenty-eight years ago; just inflation and random shootings," Amanda said, baffled.

"It was when Michael and I first moved in together."

"Wow." Amanda sat down hard on the sofa and stared out the window. "Wow. You are kidding. Right?"

Daniella sat down across from her. "Of course not. I love Michael. I miss Michael every day and this is a way to be with him."

"He's dead." Amanda stared at her. "He was my brother. I miss him too but he's dead. You need to let him go and get on with the rest of your life."

"But..."

"No buts. Going back on your own timeline is dangerous; everyone knows that. And you want to do it just so—what? You can experience poverty and youth again? You really can't be this stupid!"

Daniella colored up. If Amanda had tried to reason with her, sympathized at all, she might have changed her mind, but calling her stupid only reinforced the idea in Daniella's mind.

"Yes, apparently I am that stupid. Get out of my house. Now." She stood up and walked to the door, holding it open.

Amanda stood up, her mouth open, and she started to say something but thought better of it and just walked to the door. "I do love you, you know," she said as she walked out, and Daniella slammed the door behind her.

She arrived early at the travel center the next day. She hadn't slept so it had been easy enough to arrive first, before even the staff. She stood on the sidewalk watching a homeless man dig through a trash can for bottles. She literally ran in when the doors opened, as much for the warmth as the desire for action. She stripped down into the white robe and ran her credit card in the machine for the trip. She knew where she wanted to go for a 24-hour trip. A place her grandmother had told her about. She wanted to go to the Fillmore in San Francisco in 1968 and see the Byrds and the Grateful Dead. She told the white-coated office attendant, who wrote it down, spelling Philmore and Birds and obviously having no idea at all what Daniella was talking about.

As soon as they knocked on the smaller waiting room she walked out to the travel room.

"Why, hello, Daniella." It was the same technician as yesterday, Michael. "Did you decide to give up on the idea of going back into your own timeline?"

"Oh no. I just decided that if I had to take one trip before I go see my husband, I knew where and when I wanted to go."

"When?"

"1968 San Francisco."

"Well, that's a good choice; lots of free love and drugs. It's a popular option for many people."

"I want to go for the music."

"Sure, that's what they all say, but no one choses to go to the 1980s even if they tell me they love Michael Jackson music. No one had fun in the 1980s. It was all herpes and AIDS and getting rich on the stock market. The 60s are far more fun."

She hopped into the machine, too tired to try to explain to this peddler of depravity that she wasn't going to the 1960s for sex.

When she awoke it was 1968 and she was naked and in bed with a large hairy man. This wasn't what she wanted. She tried to scream but it wasn't her body, it wasn't her voice. She had no say in the actions of the host body she was inhabiting. The host started to nip and suck on the hairy fat nipples of this unattractive man. Daniella was disgusted and horrified. Why would anyone sign up for this? Michael had been slim and delicate and almost hairless. He had made love. This man was like an ape and he didn't make slow, gentle love. This was the mating of animals. And she could feel the host's body respond and howl and she felt an unaccustomed sensation go through her. Pleasure and lust. Danielle felt so guilty. This wasn't her pleasure or her lust, this was the lust and animalistic pleasure of her host. But it felt real—not intellectually; just emotionally and physically and chemically real. She felt alive. More than she had in a long time, more than she had since Michael had died. More than she had for years before Michael had died.

The host and her partner were finished. A joint was lit and smoked and they cuddled up together. It felt so damn peaceful. No rushing off to work, no worrying about how to pay the doctors, no worry about anything. Just the hum of a satisfied body relaxing into the bed.

Danielle wished she could control the situation. Make the body get off the bed and walk it to the Fillmore, or just out of this man's arms. But his arms were so very warm and comfortable and the breath against her neck (her host's neck, she reminded herself) felt hot and hungry. She felt both sated and sensual, and when instead of getting out of bed and going anywhere the man started to make love to her, slower this time, she could feel the love he had for her. Not her, not her, Danielle screamed. He wasn't making love to her, she wasn't making love to him. He wasn't her lover. She was just a hitchhiker in someone else's brain, but when he slid down the bed she found herself screaming her own release.

That night Donny and Maggie dressed to go out. Her host's name was Maggie, she realized as he called it again and again over and over. Maggie slid a polyester mini dress over her naked breasts and pulled on tights and thigh-high shiny plastic boots. Then she threw a fur coat over her shoulders. Real fur; an animal had died to make this coat, realized Danielle in disgust. But then when Maggie ran her hands over the fur it was so soft and lovely, and the fur surrounded her face in a sensual caress.

They walked out into the night, Donny possessively putting his arm around her shoulders. Around Maggie's shoulders, she corrected herself. And it didn't feel controlling or dominating, it felt safe and secure. And the fur coat was warm in the cool breeze the night had brought in from the ocean.

Donny had bought her dinner at a Japanese restaurant he'd picked without even asking her permission. He had ordered the sake while she'd been in the bathroom and she came back to find he had filled her a glass. They toasted together and he put his hand on her lap under the tablecloth. It was disgusting, except that Maggie didn't feel that way. She was happy and aroused and drinking more sake.

They left the restaurant, hopped on a trolley and went to the Fillmore. The technician may have sent Danielle to the body of a sex maniac, but at least he had picked someone who had been to the Fillmore the night of the Byrds' concert.

Maggie and Donny walked in and joined a group of people they knew. Maggie immediately threw her arms around a tall man-boy and French-kissed him. Donny wasn't jealous. He just squeezed her buttocks and pulled her back to him, giving her the kind of kiss that made her organs ache and was usually only delivered in private.

The music started and Danielle tried to listen while Maggie gyrated and rubbed herself against Donny. Danielle tried to look out of Maggie's eyes. Maybe she could see her grandmother. She'd said she'd been to every concert the Byrds did at the Fillmore. They had been her grandmother's favorite band. Danielle had loved her grandmother, not that she'd seen much of her the last years of her life. She'd met Michael and Michael didn't really like visiting family, not even his own. And Danielle had been so happy she just hadn't had time to see her grandmother, and then Grandma went into the home and it was so far away.

Maggie danced against Donny and he held her protectively from the crowd. He got her a beer and they smoked and drank, watching the bands play. "I can't wait to get you home," said Donny, and Maggie could feel it was true. Danielle realized that she was loving the music and looking forward to Donny taking Maggie home after the concert. She yearned to feel Maggie respond to Donny's touch. Danielle felt like a pervert and a voyeur, but she felt something and it had been so very long.

The next morning Maggie woke with her face buried in Donny's chest hair. He smelt like pot, sweat and the rum they had finished the night drinking. They were tied up in the sheets and Maggie looked over at the alarm clock. It was 8:30 a.m. Her own alarm was ringing. Danielle's 24 hours were almost over. She activated the return cycle and woke up in her own body as Maggie started to slowly kiss Donny awake.

She lay there for a moment, catching her breath, her body still full of the hormones, of the lust, or the remnants of pleasure. She found herself smiling uncontrollably because she could not be sad. The lid lifted on the travel bed and the technician was standing there. "Oh, thank God you're ok."

"Sure, I'm great. What do you mean?"

"Oh, nothing. All good. Your clothes are waiting for you in changing room six."

"Ok, thanks," she said, wondering what the problem had been. She was obviously fine. Better than fine. She didn't remember the last time she felt this good. She walked out almost dancing to the changing room.

She got home and slept like a starving person eats. Greedily and insatiably. She felt like she hadn't slept since Michael had gotten the diagnosis, since Michael had gotten ill. She was able to finally relax and go deeply unconscious, to enjoy a dreamless worry-free rest.

She woke up late in the night, ate and went back to bed. When she woke again the sun was just rising and she was filled with the tingly excitement. Today she would go back to the travel center. Today she would visit Michael.

She looked in the mirror, her smile from yesterday still fixed to her face. She asked her phone to put on 60s music and she drove to the travel office still floating. Walking into the booth, she paid for the week-long trip and walked out to give the details to Michael, the same technician who had sent her to the 60s two days before.

The technician looked scared. "I see you've already signed the waivers. I must ask you again if you are certain."

"Sure I am certain. It'll be great, just like the trip I came back from yesterday."

"Yes," he coughed. "Please make your way to the travel room."

She ran in, throwing herself down in the travel pod. "Send me, please," she asked the technician. A woman this time; she hadn't seen this one before, the white coat making her as anonymous as the other.

"I have to ask verbally if you understand the risks."

"Sure," said Danielle, impatient for it to begin. The technician nodded and the lid closed. Danielle woke standing in her kitchen cooking scrambled eggs. It was her, and it wasn't. The body felt familiar but wrong. Michael was sitting at the breakfast table waiting for breakfast, staring at his laptop screen. He looked so young, so healthy. She hadn't remembered how he'd looked then, thin but strong, his thick-lashed blue eyes so bright.

The Danielle she had once been took the toast out of the toaster and sliced the avocado next to the eggs. She placed bacon on her own plate. Michael didn't eat meat, not then, and his toast was gluten free. He was always so careful of his health, and yet... She didn't want to feel sad, she wanted to feel grateful and happy to see him.

She came over and put the food in front of him. He didn't look up. "Bon appetit," she said and started to eat.

"Could you bring me some sauce?" he asked without looking up. He hadn't even tasted the food and he was going to add hot sauce to it. She got up without complaint and got him the sauce. And also some paper towels for napkins so she was prepared when he asked for them. She sat back down to eat again.

"Thanks, love. Can I get a glass of water?"

"Sure." Of course, she'd forgotten water. She left her food and walked to get them both glasses of water.

She sat back down to eat. Her eggs were getting cold. Michael was still looking at the computer. He didn't know this was an important moment. Young Danielle didn't know it was either. Old Danielle did. She wanted more from this. This was the first breakfast after they'd moved in together. Her things were still piled in the living room. "What are you looking at?" Young Danielle asked Michael.

"Looks like the interest rates are never coming down. I don't know how we are ever going to be able to buy a house..."

Young Danielle was excited by this idea, that they would own a house together. Old Danielle remembered their first house. She'd bought it on her own credit with a deposit her parents had given her. He had never liked the house. Young Danielle reached forward and kissed him on the forehead, love in her heart.

He had cleaned up the plate. "I'm going to get a coffee. Do you want one?"

"Yes," she said, longing to go with him but looking at all the dishes she needed to do.

He smiled and went out to get her favorite drink, a vanilla latte. How long had it been, Old Danielle asked herself, since she had enjoyed a simple pleasure, like a coffee? The whole day was full of simple pleasures—unpacking her clothes into his drawers, hanging her dresses along with his suits. Cooking him dinner, sitting eating, taking their easiness together for granted.

And when night fell, getting into bed together and watching the *Late Show*. Then he made love to Danielle. And it was completely adequate. And the Danielle who had just come from the bed of Donny the hairy animal was a little disappointed. Young Danielle watched him roll over and go to sleep, then finished herself off so she too could sleep.

A week of domestic bliss and perfunctory sex followed. And then the night Old Danielle had tried to forget, the first time it had happened and he'd said it had never happened to him before. And he'd just rolled over and gone to sleep in the middle, and left her feeling so very unwanted. And she'd believed him. If it had never happened to him before, then she thought there was something wrong with her, that she wasn't sexy enough, or beautiful enough. She'd gotten out of bed to fold laundry so he wouldn't hear her cry. The week was almost up, and Danielle was ready to go home. She'd felt the love she'd always felt for Michael, but she didn't want to stay longer than the week. She'd realized she could never go back, that all the good times were best kept good and not remembered too well.

New Danielle was still unpacking on the last day. Michael had gone to work and left her there to unpack for them both. Danielle pulled out a photo album and it came open. There, Old Danielle saw a fur coat she recognized, and the person in the fur coat, she realized, was Grandma Margaret, Maggie. That was why she hadn't seen her grandma. That's why the technicians had been so upset; they had definitely made a mistake. They were supposed to send you back into the body of a DNA relative, but not one you knew. Danielle thought about her grandmother as an old woman with a cane and realized she had always underestimated her. Perhaps, Danielle thought, she had also overestimated Michael, and underestimated herself.

She woke in the travel center, the technician standing over her asking her if she was ok. And strangely enough, for the first time in a very long time, she was.

Chapter Four

NightBlind

G reg pulled her arm and she followed him, blindfold still in place. The ground was uneven beneath their feet. Where were they? Definitely off campus. He'd driven too far for it to be on campus. Outside somewhere, but where? Maybe the park. What was he planning?

She remembered when she'd been younger she hadn't understood the importance of expectation. She never wanted to wait till her birthday so she'd raided her parents' room rooting out the good gifts and taking them into her room. Her father had started to yell at her. "When I was your age we didn't have things. You take everything for granted." But her mother had stepped in. "Oh, come on, Sid. She's just excited. They're her things. Let her enjoy them." Her father had grunted and retreated into his office. When her birthday finally came the only presents she had to unwrap were the second-rate gifts she hadn't really wanted in the first place, the ones she had left behind in their room.

Her desire was building. She wanted to peek, she wanted to see where she was. She waved her free hand around trying to find a clue—nothing, no trees close by. She lay her hand against her thigh and felt her microfiber skirt swing beneath her. At least he'd let her finish getting dressed before he'd blindfolded her. She sniffed deeply and smelled nothing; just the dry, dead air of the city, warm and reused, and her own perfume. Next time less perfume, she said to herself.

Greg was still pulling her along, uphill now, her toes kicking little stones. What was he planning? Was he going to keep the blindfold on while he made love to her here? Wherever here was. She started to lick her lips while her mind filled with pictures of what he could do with her while she was blindfolded. Perhaps he'd gone in circles and even now they were in front of the In-N-Out Burger on campus, walking through the garden. Maybe he was going to make love to her there, while everyone drove by, while everyone honked and whistled and she could say she didn't know where she was while she listened to them all. All of them wanting her, all of them envying Greg, all of them moving their eyes over her naked body. It was a deliciously scary idea.

Greg stopped and pulled her to him. Everything was quiet except the sound of his voice whispering in her ear. "I love you, Emily." He wrapped his arms around her and undid the blindfold, turning her from him. They were near the Observatory, at the top of the park, and down below them lay the city. A million lights twinkled beneath her, and she was only disappointed for a moment. Then she was caught up in the beauty of the yellow lines of streetlights, the white glow of houses out as far as she could see till they disappeared into the gray night sky. Greg pulled her back towards him and whispered in her ear, "Emily, I want to give you the world. I love you so much. Will you marry me?"

She turned back to him and smiled. "Yes, I will." Greg pulled her to him, holding her tight, and she wondered what kind of ring he had bought.

He pulled a box out of his pocket. It was too big to be a box for a ring. She hoped this wasn't one of those gag gifts where there was a box inside a box. Greg must know she wouldn't like that, and he better not have bought her a diamond. "I know you don't like diamonds—you say they're blood stones—and I didn't want to buy a ring you didn't like, so this is just a gift to wear, and we'll go pick out a ring together." He pulled open the box and there lay an exquisite bracelet of interlocking gold and gemstones–sapphires, rubies, emeralds, amethysts and moonstones. Emily smiled. He was so perfect, so very perfect.

****

"You're late!" Hayden barked before she even had time to put her book bag down on the desk. He'd turned into such a drama queen ever since they put him in charge of the group.

"Yeah," echoed Sheila, looking more like a geek than ever. Her hair was puffed out around her head and her glasses hid more of her face than seemed necessary.

Hayden walked over to the desk Emily had thrown herself into. He leaned down over her like he was a teacher and handed her a photocopy. "We only have this room for an hour, you know."

"Oh, stop whining, will you? I'm here." She checked out his butt as he walked back to the front of the room. If she wasn't an engaged woman she would have to do something about him. In all honesty, he may have been the reason she'd joined the cause in the first place; he had a rugged prettiness with his long eyelashes, full lips and sharp cheekbones and jaw. Then again—she looked around—perhaps he was the reason all the women in the group had joined up.

"Well, now that you're here, Princess, listen up. We have work to do. I've given you each a copy of the plan. Memorize it and burn it. Don't email it to anyone. They can trace email. Don't tell anyone what we are planning. Don't even hint."

Emily leaned down and started reading. Damn, her contact was bothering her; she blinked a couple of times to try to focus on the page. Dear God, he'd written it by hand. It was almost impossible to read. She put her hand up to ask him a question.

"What the hell, Emily, do you think this is high school?" spat Sheila. Emily had to wonder why Sheila hated her so much. Was it just because Hayden didn't like her? If only she'd make an effort, he might like her. It was not like she needed him. She had Greg, and even if Greg didn't believe in the cause, he had great taste in jewelry. She touched the bracelet on her wrist and turned it, admiring the changing colors. What could be more beautiful than colored jewels?

"But I had a question."

"Maybe I can help you, Emily." It was Jeme. He moved his chair right next to her. She slid her chair away from him just a little. Why did nerds have to sit so close? He always spat when he spoke and she didn't need to be in the firing line. "I can explain the whole plan to you.

"We don't have time for this," barked Hayden. "You help her work out her instructions later. The bottom line is that tonight is the night. Tomorrow evening at 5 p.m. Benson Hernandez will be executed by electric chair in SAN QUENTIN. This barbarity must stop. The only way we can get our message across is by taking action." His cheeks were flushed and his eyes bright. Emily thought this was the way he would look in the clutches of passion. She wanted to see him like that, wanted to see him naked, panting, his cheeks flushed, his eyes burning into her. If only she could have made love to him before Greg proposed.

Jeme leaned over and put his hand on her shoulder. "I'll explain it all to you."

"Fantastic," she moaned. Why did everything have to be so hard? Why didn't Hayden love her? Why didn't she feel about Greg the way she felt about Hayden? Greg is such a nice guy, she reasoned, and he loves me, and I will never want for anything, and he's good in bed—not exciting or amazing, but good; good enough. She closed her eyes trying to remember how good he was.

"Meeting's over." Even with her eyes closed, Hayden's voice thrilled her.

"We've still got 15 minutes till they come for the room, Emily," Jeme said, edging himself closer to her again. She could feel him moving closer, his cold, desperate sweat oozing around his neck, trying to escape like the hairs that didn't belong to his face or his chest but were just part of his overall fur. "You're going here, with Hayden." She opened her eyes and looked down. He'd flipped over the instructions and there was a map.

"With Hayden?"

"Yes, he's your partner. We've all got one. I wanted to be with you."

Of course you did. "I got engaged today," she said, pushing her bracelet in front of his face, pushing him away with her hand.

"Oh... Congratulations." He looked down at the paper. "Why don't you just go over this with Hayden since you're doing the op with him?"

"That would probably be a great idea, Jeme. Thank you so much for your help."

Jeme pushed himself up and lumbered out of the room. Hayden was still lingering at the front of the room, putting things back in his satchel. A brown leather satchel he'd inherited from his father. Cooler than a backpack, not as stuffy as a briefcase, it was so very much Hayden.

She walked up slowly. "I hear we will be together on this."

"Yes. It's simple enough. Meet me at The Gap at Hollywood and Highland at six. We're going up into the park. When we get to the top there is a wireless transmitter we can tap into and send out the virus from there. We're going to take down the Los Angeles substation. The others are taking down Burbank, Whittier, Anaheim. Those are the controlling stations. The virus will transmit to the other substations, then, when they are all infected, they will all go down for 17 minutes. Seventeen minutes of darkness, the same amount of time they used to kill William Vandiver in Illinois. Seventeen minutes to zap someone to make sure they're dead, all the time burning. People won't be able to deal with seventeen minutes without lights, without internet, without TV. We'll really wake this city up. They need to stop murdering people in the name of justice."

He had that intense look in his eyes again and she wanted to lean in and kiss him. Instead she nodded. "See you at six."

He could have been a Gap model in the jeans he was wearing, just a little too tight and well worn; perfect, in fact. The sweet gay shop assistant who had been helping her while she shopped and killed time turned instantly from her to greet him. "Welcome to the Gap. My name is William. If there is ANYTHING I can do to help you..." Emphasis on the "anything" while William's eyes stripped the jeans off Hayden. Emily wanted to laugh, because her eyes were doing the same thing.

"Hi, babe." She walked over to him and kissed his cheek. William's eyes were burning into her now. Be jealous, she thought. I'm jealous of you. So many of the really cute boys bat for your team rather than mine.

Hayden went with the act and put an arm around her waist. "I hope you weren't planning to buy anything, dear. We are late already."

She turned back to William. "Thank you so much for your help but I've got to go." She turned into Hayden's arms and gave him a hug. "Ok, babe."

He turned and she walked nestled in his arm. She could feel every spot where his body touched hers, she could feel the rush of his blood beneath his skin and the rhythm of his breath. They walked out together and she expected him to let her go but he didn't. Snuggling into him, she wanted to make the most of this to feel everything she could. They walked outside to the street and then to a bus stop.

"Why don't we take our cars?"

"No. This way we have alibis. I bought us both tickets for the 7 p.m. movie. If anyone wants to know where we were, our cars were at the parking structure and we have parking stubs and movie stubs for the film we went to. You'd know this if you'd read the instructions."

"But then I wouldn't have the chance to ask, would I?" She leaned into him and kissed him gently on the lips. His lips opened slightly and he kissed her back. Oh God, what have I done, she thought. I'm getting married, and I kissed him, and it felt so good. It felt so good I just want to kiss him again."

"Hop on, dear." He was pushing her. She shook herself and got on the bus behind him. There were tourists on the bus, as well as the usual bus riders: smelly homeless people, Hispanic girls with their beautifully overgroomed children, and the poor underbelly of a city where minimum wage wouldn't pay for parking let alone an apartment. She felt so out of place, like at any moment everyone would stop and stare and know what they were up to. But then she realized that only the tourists looked around, and they thought she and Hayden were tourists. The regular bus riders only looked at the floor, or at their cell phone, or out the window. The regular riders rode alone no matter who sat next to them.

Hayden handed over the money like a pro and they sat. He held her hand and she took comfort in that. The enormity of what they were about to do was only hitting her now, and she was scared—scared she'd be caught, scared she'd go to jail, scared she'd lose Greg. Hayden's hand reassured her. He rose and she got off with him barely cognizant of where they were. He pushed the buzzer and they crossed the street together. She looked around. Los Feliz, below the Observatory. God, she didn't want to walk up. She'd already done her five miles today on the treadmill, and if he'd told her, well, she would have worn different shoes. She thought about telling him she couldn't walk all the way up the hill, but he was still holding her hand and if she started to argue, he'd just tell her she should have read the instructions. No, she didn't want to fight. She didn't want him to let go of her hand. And then he did let go of her hand and she stood still, looking around. A tree-lined lane, the kind of peace and nature within the city that was only found in the areas of the truly wealthy. Well-kept lawns, and green leaves overhead interspersed with bright roses and other plants grown without any thought but to their beauty. She turned to smell a rose.

"Come on," Hayden called and she looked ahead. He was unlocking the door of a car.

"You have a car here?" she asked.

"Of course. Get in." She stumbled over the verge in her platform shoes and climbed down into the car. It was a sports car—not new; classic.

"This is yours." It wasn't a question. This was his car. More than the Prius he drove to school could ever be.

"Yeah. I don't drive her much."

They drove in silence up the hill until they could see the transmitter. He parked and they walked out of the car. He had his laptop, of course, in the satchel. They walked out off the path and up to the transmitter.

"I know which wires I need to tap into. You're the lookout."

"And what do I do?"

"What do you think you do, Emily? Let me know, distract them, do whatever you have to do. If it's a guy, just show him a little leg."

"You think I have nice legs."

"You know I do. Now be a good girl and watch out for me."

Hayden climbed a few feet and started to cut into some wire sheathing. Emily hoped he knew what he was doing. She didn't want him to get fried, she wanted him to come back and tell her what nice legs she had. She watched him, her heart pounding, then he took a network cable from his bag and spliced it into the wiring and worked his way back down the tower.

He was really good at climbing. She wondered if he did rock climbing, if his arms and back were hard and strung with tight cables of muscle, and she wanted to run her hands over his shoulders, down his back, down his chest.

"We're ready. Now we wait."

"Wait," she repeated, still trying to get the image of her own lust from her mind.

"It's 6:30. We've done well. We install the virus at 7:30 and by 8 p.m. the city should be dark."

"Well, we have time to kill," Emily said, sitting down on the ground. She could see the entire city from up on this hill. All the straight lines of road were so much prettier in the dark when all they were were strings of lights. "Come sit."

Hayden stood in front of her. "I don't want to sit."

"We have an hour to kill; you can't just stand there."

"Did I hear you're engaged?"

"I don't have a ring yet," she said, standing, walking closer to him.

"But you're getting married."

"I'm not married." He cared. My God, he cared; you could see it in his face. She wasn't married, not yet—a chance for one last fling, a chance to enjoy life, a chance to enjoy herself, and what else mattered? What else was there? She stood in front of him and leaned in to kiss him. He kissed her back, fully this time, and she wanted to melt into him. She wished that they were naked already.

He reached down and slid a hand up her skirt and pulled her into his erection. She arched into him, pushing herself against him, and he walked back into her, pushing her against the transmitter tower. He pulled at her underwear and they were gone and he was inside her without foreplay, without hesitation, and she screamed his name and pushed back into him.

Later when they were done, tired and breathless on the ground, she wondered where her underwear was, and how soon until she could have a shower and wash off his goo and the leaves and twigs that had worked their way into her body and hair. He got up doing up his pants. "It's time." His voice was so normal, like nothing had changed, and he went to the laptop and pressed send for the virus.

They sat silently in the darkness waiting for the virus to work. The city lay brilliant before them, the same city she'd seen with Greg, but now—now she didn't know what to do. Hayden didn't love her—she was sure of that—but Greg did. She ran her tongue over her bruised lips, licking off the last of her lipstick and the taste of Hayden. She leaned against him and started to shiver as the night air chilled, and he put his arm around her. He had a rich, deep smell and she wanted him again.

"It should be any minute now," he said, looking at his watch while she watched the city lights twinkling in ignorance of what she had done. And then she saw it—a line of darkness, then another, and another. The plan had worked, and the city disappeared before their eyes.

And the night became dark, a blackness she had never before experienced, and above her there were white dots. Stars. She knew what they were but she'd never seen them, thousands of tiny white dots filling the sky, and as her eyes grew accustomed to the dark more appeared and she fell on her back and gazed up. Millions of specks of light, each of them a distant star, a galaxy, a solar system perhaps. And in an instant, she understood. She realized how insignificant she was.

She looked at Hayden and saw him for what he was. A selfish boy who pretended to care for a cause only to be superior. She looked at his self-absorbed gaze still looking down at the city he had turned off. She wondered how many people would die because of the power outage. How many people would be killed in a car accident in an intersection or on life support in the hospital? How many people would die in

17 minutes in a dark operating room, or stumbling about in a nursing home. She looked up at the stars and she understood.

She felt all the shame and all the guilt for sleeping with Hayden. She felt so guilty for taking the jewelry from Greg. She didn't love Greg, she wasn't even worthy of Greg. She'd never loved anyone except herself. She'd always thought her happiness was important. The million suns of a million solar systems with billions of planets twinkled down on her. The self-absorption was only possible when you believed in your own importance. Looking at Hayden she knew he wasn't important. She wasn't important. She was nothing. Yet she had been given this gift. This tiny peace of stardust to use as her vessel. The universe would keep spinning without her. Nothing she did would ever be important. And yet the universe had given her the gift of life.

She walked over to the computer and pulled the cable out from the laptop. She took the laptop and threw it down the hill.

"What the hell do you think you are doing?" screamed Hayden, and chased after his laptop in the bushes.

"Trying to become worthy," she said and walked down the road towards the city as the lights came back on and the stars faded away.

Chapter Five

HuMan

Susan knocked on the door as hard as she could. She knew the bell didn't work. It had never worked, ever. Liz opened it up after she knocked the third time. She was still in her school uniform, pen stuck in her hair. "Hi, Liz. I was hoping I could come do my homework with you." Susan rolled her eyes back towards her house two streets down. "My mothers are fighting and I just can't deal with it."

"Sure." Liz held the door wide. "Come on in."

Susan followed her in. Liz's mom Candy was in the living room, dancing around with a broom, sweeping the cobwebs out of the corners. The stereo was blasting out pop music. "Hi, Susan," yelled Candy over the sound of the music.

"Hi, Candy." Susan waved. "I'm just here to do some homework," she felt the need to explain. Other people's parents always made her feel like she needed to explain, like she was in trouble and had to come up with an excuse, that she had to make them like her, whereas at home with her own mothers she rarely cared what they thought of her.

"Come on," Liz yelled in her ear and pulled her back down the corridor to her room.

When they finally stepped inside and the door was closed, it seemed peaceful. Liz was already set up on her bed doing her homework. She had a desk, a beautiful light oak one, large, clean, well lit. Susan wished she had one like it at home, but Liz preferred to do her homework on the queen-size bed with books and papers laid out everywhere and various pens capless, leaking tiny dots onto the pink and cream quilt. Susan laid her things out on the desk and started to pull out her pens.

"So, you want to tell me about it?" Liz asked.

"Nothing to tell; just the usual. You don't mind that I came over, do you?"

"No, I love having you here."

"Thanks." Susan wished she hadn't gone home at all. She wished she'd just come straight home with Liz and called to say where she was. If she didn't study, how was she supposed to pass her year ten exams? If she didn't get her homework done, how was she supposed to keep her GPA up? How was she ever going to get to college? She wished her mothers thought about that instead of how much they hated each other. She'd heard them screaming before she'd even walked through the front door.

"Yes, I'm home from work early. I worked a double shift yesterday, remember? And since it started to rain the foreman sent us home. Can't be laying cement in the rain. And what the fuck difference does it make anyway?"

"But I don't have dinner ready and if you'd told me you were going to come home early, well, then I would have asked you to go to the store on your way home."

"Isn't it enough that I make all the money around here; now you want me to do your grocery shopping as well?"

"Megan, it's not like that. It's just that since you were on your way..." Her mom had started to cry at this point.

"Don't cry." Susan didn't have to see it; she could tell from the stifled sobs that Mum was holding Mom now. "Please don't cry."

"You don't love me anymore. I don't know if you ever did. When was the last time you took me out, or made love to me?"

"You fucking bitch, after all that I've done for you..."

It was at this point that Susan had climbed through her window with her schoolbag. She'd left a note on her desk but they wouldn't read it. They wouldn't even know she'd gone for a while. Susan knew where this one was going; it would escalate now, with both of them screaming and crying. A few more breakable items would be broken and then Mum would carry Mom into the bedroom and they would emerge in a couple of hours calm and sweet, with only a slight aroma of regret and despair. She'd be home by the time the makeup sex was over.

Susan stared at the huge pile of books she'd brought with her. History, English, Calculus and Biology homework. How was she supposed to get this all done in one night and still have time to study? She looked over at Liz, so grateful to have a friend she could come to. When she was at Liz's house she always felt at peace. She didn't need to chat to Liz, or have her talk. They had an easy silence that was rare and special. She opened up the biology book first. It was her worst subject, so she may as well do it first and get it out of the way.

Human biology, she read to herself, consists of long chains of DNA (**deoxyribonucleic acid**). As if a two-year-old doesn't know that, she thought. In the following examples of human DNA, map the genome and list the most likely characteristics of each subject.

She sighed and started. At least it wasn't too difficult. The subject had a ddATP on the 12th chromosome, and combined with the ddGTP on the 8th chromosome she would have a proclivity towards adventure. She was very tall, brown hair, green eyes, fair skin, right handed, and quite musical. She worked through her work methodically, in silence, and was so absorbed she didn't notice Liz calling her till she said her name the second time.

"Hey, Susan."

"Yeah"

"Can you come help me with this math problem?"

Susan nodded and walked over. Liz had never been good at math. Even in Year 2, Susan had had to help her with her homework. It wasn't that she was stupid; Susan knew her friend well enough to know she was quite brilliant, but not with math, not with numbers of any kind. I must ask the teacher tomorrow where I can find mathematics ability on the genome, thought Susan. It would be there somewhere, and wherever that somewhere was, Liz's Mothers had picked a different gene combination instead.

Liz scooted over on the bed and Susan lay down on her stomach beside her. They both looked down at her tiny curling script.

"It's simple, Liz. Watch. Look, you added plus 4 to this side, right? So you have to add it to the other side as well. That's what you forgot to do. Now you should be able to solve for x."

"Can you watch?"

"Ok." Slowly, in what seemed like hours, not seconds, Liz worked through the rest of the problem and came up with an answer, x=23, an answer which Susan had known just by looking at the question.

"Did I get it right?"

"Yes," nodded Susan and sat up to leave the bed.

"Stay," Liz said, sitting up to face her.

"You can do the next one without me," smiled Susan.

"That's not what I was thinking about," Liz said. Reaching her arms around her, Liz pressed her lips to Susan's. Susan sat there, still. Liz had kissed her before—pecks on the check, friendship kisses. Nothing like this. She'd felt her tongue slide in between her teeth and she wanted to pull away, pull back, but Liz's arms were still around her pinning her own down, and she was trapped. There was no way to break the embrace without hurting Liz, without hurting her friend, her best friend.

"Knock, knock." It was said after the door was opened. Liz's mother Stacy never knocked. Liz let Susan go and they both turned to look at her. "Hi, Susan. Candy was wondering if you were staying for dinner."

Susan could hear Liz trying to catch her breath. She felt breathless herself, a breathless panic. All she wanted to do was leave. Now to make her voice sound normal for Stacy, sound like herself. "No, thank you, Stacy. My mothers want me home for dinner."

"Oh, that's a pity. Well, I'll leave you two," she said, backing out and shutting the door, giving them her implicit permission to continue kissing, to make love.

"I really do have to go," Susan said, standing up.

"Can't you stay?" Liz gave her a come hither smile. "We could have fun."

"My mothers don't know where I am."

"You could call them."

"Liz, you're my best friend in the whole world and I don't want to screw that up."

"It won't screw it up. You know, my mothers were best friends in high school and they still are."

"I don't want to take a chance to mess up our friendship. Sex complicates things."

"You don't find me attractive?" Liz was starting to cry now. Little tears from the corners of her eyes rolled slowly down her cheeks.

Susan sat back down and put her arms around her friend. "You know I think you're beautiful. I've always wanted to look like you." And she had. Liz was the most beautiful girl Susan had ever seen, with auburn-red hair, milky skin and dark brown eyes. Her mothers may not have selected mathematical genius for their daughter but they had selected beauty. "You're my best friend in the world and I would do anything to make you happy, but I don't want to jeopardize our friendship. You've only just broken up with Amanda."

"I should have dated you rather than Amanda."

"I know you and Amanda had some good times. She taught you a lot, didn't she?" Susan reached over and gave Liz a tissue to wipe her nose, which was just starting to drip.

"Yes," and now the tears began to pour and Susan pulled the box over and put it on Liz's lap. Amanda was four years older than them. She and Liz had started dating two years before, when Liz was thirteen.

"You need to give yourself time to get over Amanda."

"I don't want time, I want to put her behind me. I want you to be my friend." She pulled open the drawer next to her bed to reveal her collection of toys—vibrating, spinning, strap-on. "I want you to make me scream 'till I forget about her."

Looking at all the mechanical devices had never made Susan feel aroused; instead she thought things like, when was the last time they were sterilized? Or why would anyone make anything that color? She needed to get out. She needed to get home. She didn't want to hurt Liz but she couldn't... she just couldn't. "Liz, you're still grieving over Amanda. I don't want to be your stopgap; I want to be your friend. I have to go." She got off the bed and put her things in her bag. What was wrong with her? Why couldn't she just make love to her friend, maybe marry her, have children, live happily ever after?

Liz blew her nose and looked up. "You might be right. You know, I should never have dated Amanda; I should have just waited until you were ready and started dating you."

But I am still not ready. I may never be ready, Susan said to herself. "You can't go around wishing the past was different. You're going to be fine. It will all work out." She walked over, backpack on, and went to give Liz her goodbye hug. Liz tilted her head up and clamped her mouth down on Susan's, her teeth grinding on hers, the last of her snot entering Susan's mouth. She opened her mouth from the pressure and felt Liz's tongue invade her, seeking response, seeking satisfaction. Susan wanted to kiss her back, she wanted to make her happy, but her body was just frozen, unable to flee, unable to reciprocate.

Liz pulled back and looked her over. "I know you're still a virgin but I can teach you how to kiss. I can teach you everything."

Susan bit her lip and stepped back. "See you tomorrow at school."

Liz smiled, licking her lips. "Sounds great."

Susan made herself move as slowly as she could—don't run, don't run—until she was out of Liz's house, and then she ran, wiping her mouth with her hand and rubbing it onto her shirt.

Her mothers weren't in bed when she returned. Instead they were in the living room with a drink in their hands and they looked happy. Too happy to yell at her. Too happy to yell at each other.

"Hello, Susan. Where were you?"

"Liz's."

"Oh great. Sit down, dear," said Mum.

"Yes, we have wonderful news," said Mom.

Susan sat, too exhausted to care but curious anyway.

"We're going to have another baby."

"What?"

"A baby, and I'm going to carry it this time," said Mum. "You know Mom carried you, but this time I want to feel it grow and kick and move inside me."

"But you're too old."

"I'm not too old. I'm 35; it's now or never. They won't impregnate me once I'm 36."

"But what about your job?"

"I'll take a year's maternity leave and your mom and I can just stay home looking after the baby. I'm going to go in tomorrow to start the procedure."

They both looked so happy. Susan just wanted to scream. Another baby! Another baby? They had enough trouble living together when it was the three of them and they wanted to bring another baby into it, another girl to look after, another mouth to feed when they were always saying how they didn't have enough in the first place? She was not expecting this; they were getting divorced, separated, going on vacation, anything but this. Susan stood numbly. "I still have to swot for the test tomorrow. Congratulations." She walked out to her room, shut the door and locked it.

She threw her backpack on the old kitchen table she used as a desk, then she lay down on her bed and started to cry.

"Do you know why you've been called to my office?" said the Priestess, handing her a glass of water.

"Career counseling?" Susan said, knowing it probably had much more to do with her failed test and the sick days she'd been taking off school.

"Not exactly. You've been off school a lot lately."

"Yes." Trying to stay away from Liz, making sure that she was never alone with Liz, making sure Liz's insistent kisses never went further. She didn't want to wreck her friendship; she didn't want to disappoint her. Susan had begun to wonder if it was just that she was scared, too scared. If her fear of disappointing Liz was keeping her from making love to her, if she just needed to get her virginity out of the way so at least she'd know what was expected of her.

She'd snuck out on Friday night dressed up the way young girls wanting to look older dress. Short, short skirt showing her immature long legs, a low-cut sequined blouse from her moms' closet, uncomfortably high heels and too much make-up. She got off the bus downtown. She had enough money for a cab home in her purse. She walked towards the loudest noise. It was a black-fronted building that was never open during the day, all dark, mirrored glass, but now in the night she could see the spinning lights inside. She walked in and over to the bar. "What would you like," said the bartender, a girl not much older than herself with enormous motionless breasts.

"Gin and tonic." That's what her mothers usually drank. She'd tried one once; it tasted ok.

"Four dollars." Susan slid the money across the bar, picked up the drink and threw it down like it was water.

"Could I have another, please?" she asked.

"Sure."

Susan handed over five dollars this time, leaving the change for a tip, and looked around. There were about a hundred women on the dance floor, dancing alone or with someone. She thought about going to the dance floor and dancing alone. The kind of dance that women did when they wanted attention, a pole dance without a pole, arms moving up and down their own body. But she was too shy. Perhaps later, when she was drunk. She wanted to get drunk. Drunk enough to do what she needed to do, drunk enough to do what was normal for everyone else. The first drink was making her head spin a little already. She hadn't eaten dinner, hadn't been able to. She felt someone staring at her and she turned to look at her. The woman was probably thirty, probably almost as old as her mothers, but she was beautiful. A tight firm body and golden hair and skin. Susan looked at her openly. She would know what she was doing; that much was obvious. Susan sucked down the last of the second drink and could feel it burning a warm path to her stomach. The woman was at her side. "Could I get you a drink?"

"Sure," said Susan, although the word came out slightly slurred.

"Bartender, one more of what she's having and a mojito for me." The blonde turned to Susan. She was standing much too close, the tops of her golden breasts in Susan's face, freckled and exposed. "I'm Tanya."

"Susan."

They left their drinks behind and went to the dance floor. Tanya's hands slid up and down Susan's body, and as they ground their hips together with the music Susan felt her first stirrings of excitement. Tanya could see it too. They walked back to the bar where Susan downed the last of her drink, then out to Tanya's car. Susan lay back in the car seat, her eyes closed, while the pounding music from Tanya's stereo pulsed through her. Then she felt a hand on her breast, gently circling and pinching her nipple. "We are here." Tanya's voice whispered and she got up as Tanya led her into the house and through to the bedroom, slightly stumbling as she walked.

Tanya kissed her and she fell back on the bed giggling. Tanya knew exactly what to touch, how much friction to apply, and soon her fingers were inside her and Susan was screaming in release. Then Tanya got out the equipment and Susan could feel herself going cold. She looked at Tanya's breasts and wished her breast looked like that, were that large. Maybe they were fake. Perhaps when she was older she could get fake breasts too. Tanya pushed into her, fingers, lubricant, more fingers, device. It all felt wrong, and Susan felt herself tense and tighten, fighting the sensations, feeling only fear, then pain, then numbness. Then Tanya's breast in her mouth, the breast she had thought was so beautiful, that she had wanted for herself, shoved into her throat, choking her, squashing her face. She wanted to push it away, she wanted to breathe. Then soft fingers and sharp fingernails making their way down to her clitoris again and she could feel her body responding, the same way it did when she rubbed herself there, but her mind started to yell. She wanted to leave. She hated this. She just didn't like sex. She just wasn't cut out to be anyone's girlfriend. She was going to lose Liz. There was just something wrong with her. And she began to sob, weep.

Tracy pulled back. "What's wrong? Oh baby, I didn't know you were a virgin. It always hurts the first time. If I'd known I would have kept the toys to a minimum."

"I'm sorry," Susan said. Not able to stop now, she just kept crying.

"I'll make it better," said Tracy and lowered herself down to Susan's crotch and started to lick and suck. All Susan felt was embarrassment. She'd gone to the bathroom earlier; it must all smell and taste of urine. This couldn't be how people had sex. Her mothers couldn't do this. She started to cry louder, her body shaking from the sobs while Tracy worked harder and harder on pleasing her.

"I want to vomit," cried Susan, and Tracy sat up, licking her lips. Susan threw herself out of the bed and to the bathroom. She knelt down and started to throw up, throw up the alcohol, the taste of Tracy's lipstick, the feeling of disgust and disappointment she had in herself. Tracy came and washed her face down with a wet cloth, wiping off the tears, snot and bile.

"Please, call me a cab. I have to go home."

Tracy nodded and left the bathroom. By the time she returned to say the cab was outside, Susan had washed down her legs with the wet cloth and thrown up two more times.

She grabbed her bag and walked out to the door. Tracy put her arms around her and kissed her hard as she was leaving. "You know where I live."

"Yes," said Susan and ran to the cab.

She couldn't remember the ride home. She hadn't really been in the cab; instead she'd been back in Tracy's bed, with its red satin sheets, Tracy above her, Tracy in her, and she tried to understand what was wrong with her. Why couldn't she just enjoy it? Why did she just go cold? When she got home she got in the shower and started to scrub. She stayed there washing off her own disappointment, washing off her disgust until the hot water ran out. Then she got into bed. Her body ached, and she knew in her heart that it wouldn't have been better or different with anyone else. She would only disappoint Liz, or anyone who loved her. There was just something wrong with her.

The next two days she stayed home sick, hung over from alcohol and grief.

"You failed the recent test," continued the Priestess.

"I wasn't feeling well."

"You haven't turned in your assignments for two weeks."

Susan turned and looked at her, really look at her. The Priestess was dressed in the traditional black robes (or sack, as Liz always said), her face was white, and around her eyes and mouth lines of concern and humor were well established. Her hair was black, almost as black as the uniform, out of a bottle definitely, and Susan wondered why she bothered.

"Priestesses don't marry, do they?" Susan said, mostly to herself.

"No."

"You don't have to have sex, right?"

"What is this about, Susan?"

"Well, I think I might want to become a Priestess, Mother."

"Come over here and call me Phyllis," said the Priestess, walking away from the desk and settling herself on the sofa with her cup of tea. Susan followed her and sat down. "Now, why do you think you want to become a Priestess, Susan?"

"Because I just can't do IT. I mean, well, my friend Liz... She's been my best friend since we were five and she thinks that we should, you know, and then get married. And well, I know I can't. I don't know what's wrong with me. I know it's just me, and I know I can't. I just can't." It felt good to tell someone, and Phyllis felt like a safe person to talk to. Her eyes looked wise and kind, like they had seen all the ugliness of the world and still believed it was a beautiful place. "I mean I want to; I love Liz with all my heart and I'd die for her if I had to but I just can't do IT. I know it would make her happy. I just want to run when she puts her arms around me."

Phyllis took a sip of her tea and waited to make sure Susan had finished speaking. "I know what the problem is. Can you get your file off my desk and bring it here?"

My problem is in my file? Everyone knows I'm broken? Everyone knows there's something wrong with me? She brought the file over and Phyllis patted for her to sit next to her, then she opened up the file and pulled out Susan's genome map.

"Take a look at this, Susan. You're pretty good at biology. Take a look at Chromosome 23. See that?"

"Yes. It looks different. I don't remember this from our textbooks."

"It isn't in your textbooks. And it won't be in the college ones either. Only the Priesthood knows about this variation and what it means."

"So I'm a mutant."

"No, not exactly. Ok, let's test your history a little. What is war? And when was the last one?"

"It's when people fight each other and kill each other." It seemed like a bizarre concept, but the history books all seemed to start with it. Their civilization of peace and harmony had begun after the last war. "The last one was 1800 years ago."

"Right, 1800 years ago, and in the aftermath the Priesthood came to power. We were a group of geneticists and fertility experts. Having children after the last war was difficult. The types of bombs used had caused widespread sterility. We realized that the only way to preserve the race was to improve our fertility techniques and create more women as only they could be the mothers to a future generation. The next generation were only women. No men."

"Men?"

"Yes, men, that dirty little secret you won't find in your history books, Susan. I'm only telling you this, Susan, because I think you are right, I think you should become a Priestess, and the first lesson begins today. There used to be both women and men. Humanity was never designed to be single-sex. Children were not born because you visited your temple and the local Priestess mixed your DNA till you had the characteristics you wanted then inserted a zygote in your womb. Children were created by the act of a man and a woman making love."

Susan felt a great shudder go through her, an awakening of something she'd always felt, something incomplete, something she yearned for.

"Men provided the seeds and women the eggs. The only problem with this system is that men were genetically predisposed to fight, use violence and start war, and no one wanted another war. There were many more women than men when it came to a vote, and we'd genetically altered most of them, changing their 23rd chromosome in a way you now think is normal. These women did not need a man to be sexually satisfied, and so the vote passed. Men would be phased out. We collected seed from every man in existence and then just stopped manufacturing them."

"So they all just died?" Susan said, filled with a sadness she couldn't understand or voice.

That was the plan. It was 50 years later when we realized that we couldn't store the seed indefinitely. We thought we could, we thought we could keep it on ice and have enough that it would be millenniums before we'd need to create a couple of men to keep from running out. But in a mere 50 years it all went bad, lost its potency. We scoured the world for a man, a man who wasn't sterile and was still alive. We found twenty. They were the start of ADAM."

"Adam?"

"Agency Designation All Male. We gave them an island and created a rural lifestyle, farming and hunting, very primitive, the kind of lifestyle best suited to using their violence and energy."

"But what about when they died?"

"We gave them wives, Priestesses with the same chromosome 23 as yourself. They supervised seed collection and had children naturally. When they had children the boys stayed on the island and the girls were sent to the priesthood. There are 10,000 people on the island now, 5,000 men."

"I don't understand."

Phyllis went to the shelf and pulled a book. The wall opened up revealing a doorway.

"Come with me," Phyllis beaconed. Susan followed her into a private screening room. Phyllis touched a button and the door closed behind them and the only light was the pictures on the screen. There on the screen were men. Susan found herself drawn to the screen, to touch the moving images.

There on the screen was an old-fashioned looking village. Men and women were traveling by horseback, riding in carriages. Men were cutting wood, fires were burning in fireplaces. There were no electric wires. No cell phone towers, no signs of technology. A woman came out of a house and pumped water by hand into a bucket to bring into her house. She was pregnant and stretched backward before grabbing the bucket. An infant man-child sat on the porch calling for his mother to come back to him.

Susan reached out to the screen to touch the man-boy. His father walked out and grabbed the water off his wife and kissed her face. Susan ran her fingers down his image. Down the strangely angular face on the screen. "You're sending me to the island?"

"If you want to go," Phyllis said, smiling through her eyes.

Susan nodded, a smile stretching her lips. "I think I'd like that. It looks like home."

Chapter Six

Troll Hunt

"Konnie, have you loaded Momma's gun?" The eight-year-old nodded and handed over the shotgun to her mother with both hands, her blonde curls bobbing as she did so.

"I want to go too, Mom," whined Elizabeth, the eldest, while she loaded the reserve magazine for the AK47. "You know I'm a good shot."

Mary walked to her and ran her hand down her silky black hair. "I know you're a good shot, darling, but it's just not safe. You need to stay here and protect your sister."

"But she can shoot them with the Gatling gun if they break down the door. She knows how to use it."

"Honey, it's really dangerous out there. When you're 16 you'll have to go—I won't have any choice but to let you go—but you're only 12." She bent down and looked in her resentful preteen's eyes. "Don't be in such a hurry to grow up." She kissed her on the forehead and stood up. "You have got your 45 ready?"

"Yeah, duh."

"Ok. Look after your sister. I've got to go join the hunt."

Elizabeth checked the ammo feed of the Gatling gun as Mary went to the door. She shut the metal door, then pulled the bars across and locked them. The kids were secure in the panic room. Mary walked out to the front door and unlocked the door and the bars, then relocked them. The guard dogs sniffed her as she walked out.

"Protect my babies," she asked the dogs and the universe and walked down the street to meet her friends at the coffee house. The sun was moving lower in the sky and the Trolls would be out as soon as the sun set.

She walked as quickly as she could, moving the shoulder holster so it wouldn't rub on her bra strap. Her eyes were on the horizon as she walked, looking for signs they were coming, and she wished she was stronger. Later in the hunt when she'd used some of the ammo and the adrenalin was pumping she wouldn't notice the weight, but right now she wished she could just drop some of the armaments.

The girls were all lined up outside the coffee house like always. Maybelline was standing on a table, leading the charge. She was sixty but always a lady in her heels and lipstick. It was said she'd shot six Trolls in a row pivoting on a stiletto heel, all without smudging her mascara.

"Ok, ladies. It's full moon tonight. You all know what that means." The group grunted. "Yes siree, darlings, should be good hunting. There'll be more of them and what's more, visibility's great for baggin' yourself a collection. Go to it, girls."

Amanda beckoned Mary over. "Mary, over here. Want to go shoot the barrows tonight?"

"Yeah, sure." She hadn't been out on a hunt in almost a month, not since the disastrous last one, and she found herself a little scared.

"Heard the Trolls were busy building themselves little caves in the side of the barrows, so I say we best ought to evict em."

"How's your girls?"

"Good. My Angela's graduating high school this year. Pretty soon she'll be out with us. Then I'll just have Brenda look after the other five."

"Angela's out of high school already? Damn. Time flies. Elizabeth wanted to come tonight herself. I told her to not be in such a hurry..."

"Besides, how can she? I mean, it's just her guarding your youngest. You know I wish you'd bring your girls over to my place; they'd be safer together and if anything happened... Not saying that it will but... You heard about Jenny's girls."

"Yeah." Mary shook slightly at the thought. The Trolls had dug their way through the roof into their cellar safe room and raped all three of the girls. Mary sent another prayer out to the Universal Mother to keep her children safe.

"It's not like it isn't bad enough when one of the hunters gets raped. Damn, I shouldn't have said that. So bloody insensitive... I'm putting my foot in it ever more, aren't I?"

"It's ok," said Mary.

Amanda pulled down her night vision goggles and pointed, smiling.

Mary opened fire without thinking about it, then she slid on her night vision goggles and looked to see what she'd done. Two Trolls down. They went to look at their handywork. The Trolls lay there, shattered, their shiny bald heads and blue inked bodies hideous, with strange tribal markings on their arms, backs and chests.

"Good start, girl. Let's go find some more." Mary smiled, her fear gone, the weight of her equipment no longer bothering her. By dawn they'd neutralized thirteen. They'd caught two of them hiding in a cave house. The walls had been covered in obscene pictures. Mary had blushed and looked away. When they walked out of the cave, Amanda had thrown in a grenade. "'Cause no one needs to see such filth." The site of the burrow imploding in on itself made Mary smile. No one else would ever have to see those pictures—naked women and Trolls touching each other.

The hunt was over for another night. Amanda walked back, her night vision goggles off, the red lines of them drawn into her face. "You know, at some point we're going to run out of Trolls."

"How?"

"Well, we've got all these weapons now and we can kill so many more every hunt than our grandmothers and great-grandmothers used to do with just knives and spears. And since the ultrasounds have started on the fetuses, there are just less of them being born."

"I suppose so," said Mary, and then she looked out and saw smoke rising. Smoke rising from where her house was, smoke rising from where her children were. And she started to run.

The front door was gone—grenade maybe, or C4. The door to the panic room had been blown too.

"Elizabeth, Konnie!?" she started to scream before she even got through the front door. "Elizabeth, Konnie!?"

"Yeah, Mom," answered Elizabeth, coming out covered in filth, with the same tone of voice she would have used to answer a question about homework.

Mary dropped her guns and ran to her, catching Elizabeth in her arms. "Are you ok, my darling? And Konnie..."

"I'm fine, Mommy," said Konnie, coming out of the corner of the panic room with blood covering her hands.

Mary grabbed up her daughter's hands and started to look for damage. "Don't worry, Mom, it's not hers. She's just been poking the body."

"The body?"

"Yeah, the Troll I shot. Come look."

Mary walked into the panic room and there were the pieces of the Troll ripped apart by the Gatling gun. The legs looked as if they still wanted to walk away while the eyes stared at her from the round bald head.

The Troll was familiar. It had been years since she'd seen him, but she knew him. They had grown up together, played as children. Until one day he started to transform into the Troll in front of her and her mother had sent him out of the house at gunpoint before the transformation was complete. Before the hair grew on his face, before the lust had endangered her daughter. Mary remembered her mother crying as she pushed him out into the night. He was crying. Mary hoped the baby she was sure she was carrying was a girl. She didn't want to have to do what her mother had done. She lent down and closed the eyes of the Troll, the gray-green eyes the same color as her own, the eyes of her brother Jim.

Chapter Seven

Prostitute 732

S he walked out into the darkness and kicked her little toe on the corner of the coffee table. "Oh fuck," she moaned and swung in the darkness away from the table, and waved her arms around until she reached a table lamp. She turned it on and looked down. The toe was red, but it was still pointing in the right direction. Fuck, it hurt. Maggie reached down and touched it gingerly. It was starting to swell already. By morning it would be the size and color of a Roma tomato. Oh well, there wasn't anything the doctor could do. It was just a toe; it would heal.

If only it wasn't so dark at night, or in the daytime for that matter. She really had to buy a verbal cue module for her household computer. But how the hell she was ever going to get an extra 1000 credits together to get one was beyond her. Maybe one of her clients could get her a pirated copy; that shouldn't be more than 250. If she did a couple extra tricks this week, and didn't tell the boss about them, maybe she could get it.

She limped over to the freezer and pulled out some perma-cold cubes and tied them to her toe with a dishtowel. Damn it. She looked at the clock on the wall; 2 p.m. It was time she started getting ready for work. First shift would be off at three. She looked around the apartment. Three years here. Three years. It was so sparse. What did she have to show for all her work? What had she spent her money on? Not on new furnishings, that was sure. The same drapes covered the same non-existent windows. The coffee table she'd just broken her toe on was the same one she'd sworn she'd replace the first time she'd seen the apartment; it was one of those glass and metal ones that always looked dirty where every little smeary fingerprint could never be removed properly. In fact, she was sure she could still see the outline of the buttocks of last month's customer, one of those hairy office types who make tons of money. He'd paid for the whole night and his greasy little posterior had guaranteed she was never going to eat another meal at that table. Not that she had a kitchen table. There wasn't room enough for it, so for the last month or so she'd eaten her meals standing over the sink. At least it saved on the cleanup.

She limped into the bathroom. The vapor shower wet her and turned off. She soaped herself up and it came back on just long enough to rinse most of the soap off. She could remember before she came, when she was young, back on

Earth. She'd thought nothing of standing under the shower for half an hour. The water running down her back, down her hair. Her hair would be soaked, so wet that even after the towel she'd need a dryer to get all the water out of it.

She pulled the static brush through her hair. It would take out most of the dust; that was all she could do until the middle of the month. Twice a month she'd splurge and buy an extra gallon of water. Her routine never varied. She would pour it, the meter clicking, into a bucket. Then she would put it in the middle of the bathroom and just stare down into it, seeing her own reflection shimmer in its clarity. Then she'd plunge a hand in and wipe the water over her face. Not a lot; just enough that her face felt damp. Then she'd enter the vapor shower and get her hair damp enough to apply the soap. She'd have the water in a bowl. It would be the perfect warmth she wanted, heated on the stove until it steamed. Then she would insert her head and use her fingers to massage the water in and the soap and dirt out. Then, after her hair was wet, each strand absorbing enough water that it was heavy and sticky, she would tip the water out over her naked body and watch it run down her breasts, over her stomach and down her thighs. Sometimes a drop would lodge in her bellybutton, and she would shake with the excitement, watching the drop slowly leave and drip down between her legs and away.

Her clients had learned to accept that on hair-washing day she wasn't available. She would go to bed with wet hair and lie alone, wet and damp and cool on her own sheets, spread out on the bed she shared with so many. And while she was wet she would touch herself the ways she wished others touched her. She would finally fall asleep damp, wet, exhausted and satisfied, knowing that the next day she would have to work once more.

She put on a robe—not quite sheer but sheer enough—and turned her red light above her door on. The first client entered at 3:01; he'd either gotten off early in order to beat the rush to her door, or he'd been working in a tunnel nearby. She would have guessed the latter. He didn't look like he could violate regulations any more than any of them could. His shirt was open; it was filed with dust the way they always were. He was one of the younger models. There weren't many scars on him yet. The older ones were more beaten up.

She walked over to him to help him undress. The faster the better; there would be another 50 waiting outside the door.

"You don't have to. I'm not here for that." She stood back and looked at him. She must not have heard him right. It wasn't like they spoke. Well, they sort of grunted every word in a loud enough volume to be heard over the jackhammers.

"I am not here for sex," he said, making it clearer and sitting down.

She found herself scared. If he didn't want sex, what did he want from her? She peered down at his tag. "Number 4B8929, what are you here for?"

"My name is David."

"Your people don't have names."

"We will all have names by tomorrow night."

Maggie sat across from him. She didn't know what to do. She was ill at ease with her clothes on and no function. They'd always been so predictable. She looked across the table. Why was this one different? They weren't supposed to be different.

He looked just like all the rest, 6'8", 230 pounds, solid muscle, purple skin, hair, eyes, large dexterous hands—the perfect clone, specifically engineered for the heat, for the lack of water, for the hard manual labor. Designed to follow orders, designed not to be too intelligent, with an almost in-satiable sex drive that could be used against him. After all, the

Company provided his only female companions. There were never any females of his own species, and they were all sterile and could only be recreated in a laboratory. Perfect Company men—no, perfect Company machines with numbers instead of names, but his one was talking as if he didn't belong to the mold at all.

"I will explain," he grunted. "The end has come. You must decide tonight if you are going to leave or stay."

"Leave? I can't leave; I have a ten-year contract with the Company."

"I'm sure the Company will let you fulfill your contract on another planet. As of tomorrow night, this will no longer be a Company outpost. We will no longer be mining for the Company."

"I don't understand." She felt like the idiot now. She was supposed to be smarter than the clones, but she couldn't make head nor tail of what he was saying. Not a Company outpost? That made no sense. The Company ran everything, the universe.

"The time for revolution has come. By tomorrow evening all Company officials will be dead or fleeing the planet. There are two hundred of us to every one of them, and our lives are less important to us than theirs are to them. We die every day just by reporting to work. We will win; history teaches us this."

"You know history?

"Your choice, Maggie, is whether you stay with us here or flee with the Company ships. If you want to leave with the Company ships you will need to be in the headquarters by 11 a.m. After that I cannot guarantee you safe passage."

"Why are you doing this?" Why are you telling me? Why do you think that I won't go and tell the officials and they will send in the army tonight? Why are you trusting me? Why are you giving me this choice?

"We are doing this because we want freedom. We don't want to be Company property anymore. We thought you would understand this."

She looked around. There was nothing of her in this place. It was the Company's house, the Company's coffee table, the Company's bed where she fucked the Company's men just enough to afford to buy the Company's food and the Company's water. "I won't tell them what you are planning."

"We knew you wouldn't, Maggie." There was a tender note in his voice, and she looked over at him. He was fully aroused but not approaching her. She'd never seen a man holding himself back before. It made her feel loved. Had she made love to him before? Was he one of her regular customers? She had no idea. There was nothing about him that was unusual except that his penis was covered by cloth.

He stood and walked towards her. So now she'd have to fuck him. Well, it better be fast; they'd wasted too much time talking.

He put his arms around her and kissed her gently on the top of the head. "Goodbye, Maggie. I wish you well."

He let go of her and walked to the door, letting himself out. This goodbye had been so final. He was expecting to die during the revolt. She walked to the door to let him out. She saw a line of customers standing waiting. She looked at the first one. He looked exactly like David. But he never looked at her face the way David had. He just looked at her body and she was not Maggie; just Prostitute 732. She turned her red light off and locked her door. She heard a groan and someone knocking but she was done. Tonight everything was changing.

She walked into the bathroom and put the plug in. She turned on the tap and could hear the meter clicking. Someone was knocking on her door but she focused on the water pouring down into the bath. She thought about the Grand Canyon;

she'd seen it as a child. A trench carved into the earth by just a little water. One should never underestimate the power of a little thing. She lowered herself into steaming water. All the little things that had led her here to this time and place were over. She'd stopped dreaming things could change, but as the water swirled around her she realized things were always changing. It was she herself who had stopped and held herself still. She splashed some water out of the bath and giggled. The new world was coming and she would flow with it.

In the distance she could hear explosions. The revolution had begun, and she hoped that by the end of it both she and David would be free.

Chapter Eight

Human Contact

S he woke up dreaming about him again. His hands covered her body, and his kiss was tender, sweet, warm. She reached for him and pulled him down to her. She ran her fingers through his sun-bleached hair, just a little too long. His green eyes full of desire, he kissed her neck and whispered, "I love you, Alicia." Then his face began to peel off, revealing metal and wire. She started to scream.

The screaming woke her and the lights came on, sensing her motion. He ran into the room. "Ma'am? Are you all right?"

She nodded and sat on the edge of the bed trying to catch her breath. She stared down at her toes. She couldn't look at him. She couldn't see him in his uniform looking so calm, professional, robotic. She wanted to remember him the way he was at the start of her dream.

"Could I bring you anything, Ma'am? Chamomile tea perhaps?"

"Yes." She watched him as he left. He was beautiful. He'd been a part of her life forever. She couldn't be thinking about him this way.

"On screen," she said and the wall lit up. She selected a classic film she'd never seen and pulled up her e-mail—just junk and bills. She clicked back and forth between the mail and the movie, not paying attention to either. Marcus would look after the bills for her, the way he looked after everything... everything except the emptiness inside. She had hoped there would be a mail from a friend, from her mother, from someone. It was so long since she had seen anyone, touched anyone. She got out of the bed and looked at herself in the mirror. She pulled the skin around her eyes. It wasn't as firm as it had been. She felt old.

"Ma'am. Here is your tea."

"Thank you, Marcus. When was the last time my mother visited?"

"In the flesh, ma'am?"

"Yes."

"Twelve years, three months, eight days. Her apartment was hit by a direct missile attack and the hermetic seal was broken. She was here for three days while her apartment was repaired and sterilized."

"Did she touch me?"

"Touch you? Are you all right, ma'am?"

"Yes, sure."

She needed people. She plugged into the virtual world, and went shopping. There were others there, some real, some computer generated, moving around in a simulated mall. She stood in line for a movie and looked around. She must be able to find someone to be with, someone attractive, someone who was looking for her. She'd read enough books, seen enough movies; they all talked of love. If everyone else spoke of it then it must exist. And if there was love then somewhere someone was right for her. She looked around again. An overweight woman of color behind her was talking with one arm stretched toward the prune-skinned matron whose mottled skin looked like a mask. In front of her a cute dark-haired man with artistic and slightly insane whiskers was staring at his cell phone rather than look at anyone around him. But both the woman behind and the young man had left her six feet of space. She looked up and down the line. Groups of two, three, and singles lined neatly, closely, but around her there was no one.

It must be her. She must be creating an invisible shield that kept others out. There must be someone she could love, someone she could let in. She didn't want a shield. She wanted to be held, shielded, loved. There must be someone for her. What if she had missed him, what if he had given up and settled for someone else? Three people down stood a candidate; long black hair hung down around the bluest eyes. But she knew she would say nothing to him. She had always been alone and always would be, no matter how many people stood about.

She plugged out of the virtual world without seeing the movie and lay down in the simulator. She attached the electrodes and programmed in the looks of the boy she had seen in the line. "Fantasy 13," she told the machine, but as her eyes saw the young dark-haired man ripping her clothes off she found herself thinking of Marcus. Her desire overwhelmed the programming, and picking up on her brainwaves the image in front of her changed to Marcus.

His green eyes full of desire, he kissed her neck and whispered "I love you, Alicia." She reached for Marcus. His face froze into a mannequin, and she began to scream.

He ran into the room, and helped her pull her naked body from the machine. "Ma'am? Are you all right?"

She was blushing. Sitting on the edge of the bed trying to catch her breath, she stared down at her toes. She couldn't look at him. She couldn't see him in his uniform looking so calm, professional, robotic.

"Please leave. I am fine," she said and he walked away. She grabbed for her robe and put an emergency call into her doctor.

"That's why I needed to see you, Doctor. I don't know what's going on with me. I keep dreaming about Marcus."

"Marcus, your servant?" He was punching the information into his computer looking for the answers to come to him.

"Yes."

"The medication has not mitigated your symptoms?"

"No. I can't concentrate on work, or anything."

"This may be the start of an obsession. Have you been utilizing the simulator as prescribed?"

"Yes, but it isn't just sex. I want him to hold me. I want someone to hold me, to love me. I want human contact."

Doctor Yae scowled. "You know how dangerous contact is; I don't need to tell you how irrational you are being. I will send over some more medication." Some medication, some pills—that was the standard response. Didn't he understand? A couple of pills wouldn't fix it. Loneliness couldn't be cured by drugs.

"Ok." She hung up and walked into the kitchen. Marcus was working at the stove, his lithe grace both efficient and effortless. She watched him beat the eggs; they would be perfect, as always. She couldn't stop watching him. She wanted him to watch her, and she was worried about her sanity.

Marcus put the food on the table. She pulled up a screen rather than look at him. She put a call in to Kelly, her best friend. She and Kelly had been friends since they were children. They had been to elementary school together before the epidemic, then they had been to virtual high school and had even taken the same virtual classes at college. Kelly's specialty was hardware, advanced nano-engineering for industrial robotic applications. Alicia had always been more interested in programming.

"Hi, Alicia. How're you doing?" Kelly smiled. She was getting older too, Alicia noted. When the smile left her face the lines didn't disappear.

"Have you got some time?"

"Yeah."

Alicia walked into the bedroom and shut the door. Marcus wouldn't care. She could have even ordered him not to listen but she was embarrassed about him hearing. It didn't make sense, but nothing made sense anymore. She looked at the floor and told Kelly as quickly as possible, "I'm obsessed with him."

"Not him," responded Kelly. "It. He's not a him, he's an it."

"I know that. You don't have to remind me."

"Is he an anatomically correct model? You know I could fix him if he isn't."

"Dear God, Kelly..." Alicia started to blush.

"Look, you aren't the first person. I mean, sometimes the simulator isn't enough. I modified one of my own..." Kelly had always been more adventurous than Alicia. Alicia remembered when Kelly had hacked into the school's central computer and added a degree in Kissing to the curriculum.

Her justification had been that kissing was a dead art form that had had the power to change the course of wars, and yet no one did it anymore, or knew how.

"I want him to love me..."

"He's a robot, Alicia. I can fix the equipment, but you want love?"

"Yeah."

"Well, you're the programmer. Just write an emotional sub-routine."

"Don't you think it's weird I want a robot to love me? I'm so miserable I almost called my mother."

"Your mother? That witch?"

"She is my mother, and she's a genius." Alicia felt the need to defend her, even now when they barely spoke and most of their conversations ended in argument.

"Do you remember your 10th birthday party? She never even came; too busy, she said. Then your 11th..."

"I don't need to be reminded. I've spent enough money telling my therapist. Damn, I'm so lonely. Maybe it's just a biology thing. Maybe if I could have a child..."

"None of us can have children." The smile faded from Kelly's face and she just looked sad. "Just get busy with your robot and take the doc's pills. I have to go, but I'll call you tomorrow."

"Thanks, Kelly." The screen went back to the entertainment selection.

There was a knock on the door. "Ma'am? Would you like fish or chicken for lunch?" It was Marcus, and she wanted to see him. She ran to the door and opened it.

"Marcus, could I speak to you?"

"Of course, ma'am."

"Come here." She took him by the hand, walked him to the bed, sat him down on the edge and sat next to him. "Marcus, you've been with me a long time."

"Your whole life, ma'am. Your mother constructed me twelve years before you came into existence."

"Please call me Alicia."

"Yes, Alicia."

"I want you to care for me."

He looked at her with his warm green eyes, sun-bleached blond hair, eternally young, a man-child who would never fill out, a freshness that would never fade. His hair looked soft and she reached out to touch it. He moved slightly and her fingers grazed his cheek.

"But I do care for you, Alicia. Don't I take care of everything you need?"

She started to blush and he put his arms around her, and held her like one would hold a child. She kissed him on the lips tentatively, exploratorily, questioningly. His lips were warm, slightly open, and she tried to remember what Kelly had told her about kissing but she could remember nothing. She could just feel with an elated panic her body respond and her arms clenching him tighter.

"I want you," she said as he pulled away from the kiss, watching her. "Please."

"I would like to make you happy, Alicia, but are you sure?"

"Yes."

"You say that now, but I'd like you to think about it. I need to do some shopping." He stood and drew one finger down her cheek. "We will talk when I return."

He walked away and she followed him to the door. He leaned down and hugged her, then walked through to the decontamination lock. She watched him remove his indoor clothes and put on his outdoor suit. She'd seen him change a million times but now the sight of him filled her with guilty excitement.

Marcus frowned to himself as he walked out of the building and down to the town. He nodded as he passed other servants escaped from their apartments to the outside. The sun was shining, and the cafés were full.

"Hey, Marcus." It was Sylvia, the mail carrier. She ran over and gave him a kiss on the cheek. "The master let you out, did she? What are you doing this evening?"

Sylvia would never understand. He looked around him at the cars on the street and the shops, restaurants, bars, cinemas, all thriving, full of customers—all things that Alicia had never seen, a life denied to humans. "I'm in a hurry, Sylvia. Maybe later."

"Doesn't she understand you need some time off? She can't need you all the time?" She placed her manicured hand on his arm.

"Actually, she does. Now, excuse me." Marcus pulled himself past her and walked away. Sylvia could never understand; she was too young. She'd never spent any time with humans. Marcus ducked into the supermarket where Sylvia would never follow him and grabbed a tub of Chunky Monkey, Alicia's favorite ice cream.

He walked out into the street looking both ways for Sylvia. The street was full of beautiful, youthful, flawless robots going about their lives. He walked down to a quiet café and pulled into a booth at the rear. He activated the screen. It was easier to distance himself from her if he only saw her image and didn't project his image into her home. He dialed her number.

"What is the password?"

"The password is darling."

"Hello, Marcus." She looked bad, worse than the last time he'd seen her. Her body seemed to be shrinking, as if the tubes were draining the life from her rather than keeping her alive.

"Hello, darling. Can I come see you?"

"The doctors would never allow it. I want to live as long as I can; the less stress the better. At least we can still talk."

"I still love you."

She smiled, her gray, lined face folding into her skeleton. "You didn't call to tell me what I already know, my love, so what's happening with Alicia?"

"The latent programming is coming into play."

"The love subroutines?"

"Yes, and since I am the only person with whom she associates..."

"She's my daughter. I want what's best for her, and you were the best. My greatest love and the best lover I could imagine." She started to cough. It was a weak cough yet it shook her bony torso. She caught her breath like a drowning man. "I know you'll make her happy in a way that I never could. I never seemed to be able to do the right thing for her."

"You tried. But maybe the mistake was treating her like she was human."

"I didn't know what would happen with my species. I knew I was having problems conceiving, and so did my friends, but we never realized that the bio-weapons had already destroyed the next generation."

He'd heard these arguments before. He'd agreed with her once. "Don't give me your justifications. Alicia was just a salve to your pride, a child when others couldn't have them, something to show off at the parties."

"Yes, my perfect husband. Then our perfect child grows up to hate me and only know you as the butler."

He wanted to reach out and touch her. She looked so frail he wasn't sure if he would kiss her or hit her. He loved her so much, yet she'd kept their child contained by the lifestyle of a dying civilization.

"I know it was wrong, Marcus, I know that now, but I don't know how to change it. I can't just destroy her image of herself. You remember what happened to Christine?"

Of course he remembered; no one had ever given him the capacity to forget. Christine's death was still fresh. Even a robot couldn't survive jumping from a fifty-story building. He hoped she'd found the heaven she'd believed in. "Ok, so we can't tell her. What do you want me to do?"

"Be there for her, Marcus. You can't be her father, but you can be her husband."

"I don't know if I can. I love you. It feels so..."

"You never were good at following orders. Marcus, when you return home, run subroutine 893. It will let you forget me."

"Maggie, I don't want to forget you. I want to talk to you every day till you die."

"And I want to speak to you, but for once I want something for someone else more. I want Alicia to be happy. I know you could be happy with her. If you run the subroutine then you'll have only been my ex-servant, now Alicia's lover, and when I call her we can speak."

"As strangers, I can speak to that hologram you let her see of you, that woman who is healthy and young."

"In my world everyone is healthy and young, Marcus. I made this world."

"And then trapped our daughter outside it."

"I can't change that. Please help me make her happy." She started to gasp for air. One of her nurses came in and the screen went blank.

Marcus walked home. Before he entered the house he could see Alicia at the window, watching for him. He walked into the decontamination room and started to strip, shower and change, going through all of this as part of the farce. This time it was different. She watched him with hunger and uncertainty. He stood there naked, embarrassed. He'd thought all the way home. She was so human. Programmed to age, she looked just like her mother had when she'd made him. He had loved Maggie so, despite her selfishness, despite her arrogance, and she still loved him, loved him enough to give him this second chance at happiness. "Run subroutine 893," he said quietly, and in an instant, it was done. He put on his clothes, picked up the ice cream, and stepped into the kitchen.

Alicia sat waiting, biting her nails, awaiting his return.

"Well, have you decided?" asked Marcus.

"Yes," she said. "I love you, and I want you." She ran to him and put her arms around him. She kissed him softly on the lips.

He entwined his arms around her, reached down and kissed her neck. "I love you, Alicia." He picked her up and carried her to their room.

Later he would ask for the things he needed, later he would find a way to take her out of the house into the world, later he would ask permission to die with her, later they would have a child. Kelly would help them, the way she had been programmed to. There was time for everything later.

Gluttony

Chapter Nine

The Traveler

C harlotte always found the uniformity of airports decep-
tive, as if she hadn't really gone anywhere at all but was
right back where she had started, wherever that may have
been. When she was younger she'd loved everything about
traveling, even the jetlag; just being able to go somewhere else
was all she had needed. She'd spent so much time in airports,
but since 9/11 it had only gotten harder, more tiring, less joyful.

She let the crowds go fight for a line at Immigration and
went into the restroom, which was vaguely familiar. She'd definitely been here sometime; the pale lime tiles and self-flush-

ing toilets resonated a memory, but she didn't know when, or where she'd been coming from or going to.

The line was halfway back to the plane by the time she joined it. Humanity in bulk, reduced to a herd of cattle, easily led, manageable. As individuals they might be interesting, like the blonde woman in front of her—bleached hair, gray suit, four-inch heels, small waist and sun-ravaged face. Charlotte had been on the plane with her from Costa Rica. So what had she been doing in Costa Rica in a gray suit, and why was she flying in heels? The suit was off the rack and fit well across the shoulders, but the sleeves were a little short, and it was polyester. A polyester gray suit in Costa Rica. Charlotte would have been sweating, but not the aging blonde. She looked as cool as her perfectly coiffed hair; perhaps a sales rep.

And over there, the giant boy, at least 6'9", with the old man, obviously his boss, both of them in the cheap, ill-fitting suits of insurance salesmen or Mormon missionaries. Sweat ran down the boy's face as he melted beneath his suit.

The tourists in front, old enough to be enjoying their retirement, not talking about where they had been or what they had done but instead discussing the film they'd seen on the plane, as if that were more important. She knew when they got home and talked about their trip, that would be one of the first things they mentioned. The movie would have been cheaper in the theatre.

Charlotte realized that she loved humanity, wanted to know their stories. She wanted to know everything about all of them, liking nothing better than people-watching—to overhear them talk, to watch them move about. But she didn't feel like one of them. She didn't feel like she belonged to the same species. She wasn't one of the cattle. She considered for a moment breaking all the rules and just running over to the air crew and diplomat line, leaving these thousands of herd animals chewing their cud, their destinies directed by red rope lines.

She considered it, then thought better of the fleeting impulse. Not because she was afraid of consequences—what could they really do to her—but because it was more fun to stand in line watching the creatures for the two hours till her next flight.

Charlotte was returning home to Los Angeles. Home; what a strange concept. Yes, she'd been born in Los Angeles, and her family was there, but home was an idea, an abstraction, something she wanted but had never found. The last couple of years in Costa Rica had been fun, but like every other place she found herself in, it hadn't been home. She'd traveled the world working where she could, paying her way as she went, looking for something—a sense of belonging, a sense of peace. But much like love, she'd given up on finding it.

She knew what awaited her here. Her mother, growing angrier and more frustrated with age. "How long are you going to be home this time?"

And her father, the hero of her youth. "Hello, my darling. How are you doing? Why don't you settle down here for a while?"

And it was tempting to just relax, rest, stop moving. But she could only do it for a time before the empty ache would drive her forward on her quest for a place where she belonged, a place where she could be herself, a place where she didn't feel like an alien. She desperately wanted to find her true home.

In all the years of traveling she'd met others. Shadow people who lived ephemeral lives without ties, mortgages, careers—the best word she'd ever heard to describe them was travelers. Other people were tourists; they went to places to tour and be shown something. Travelers went in search of a deeper truth, the elusive sense of "home." A traveler wouldn't come to Italy to do the usual attractions; they would unpack their backpack, start work wherever. They could stay until either their money, visa, or love of the place ran out. A traveler would stay until some other place beckoned.

Charlotte reached for her bag on the turnstile. Just the one; it was all she owned—that and a storage unit in LA. She swore one day she'd burn everything in that storage unit: all the old clothes, yearbooks; all the memories. Either that or move it into her home—if and when she finally found it and settled down.

She heard her mother before she saw her. "There she is, Peter. See? Over there. I told you, over there. Look how skinny she is. Oh my God."

She turned and walked toward her parents; her mother's shape had less definition every time Charlotte returned, while her father seemed to vanish a little, year by year. She could barely see in him the man who had thrown her in the air and swung her onto his broad shoulders to get a better view of the world. He had become a bent gray figure, slowly fading from her sight.

"Oh Charlotte, you're so thin. What have you been eating?"

"Food, Mother."

"Not real food. It's probably been that rice and beans junk. You know a mother can tell. A mother can tell, can't she, Peter?"

"Yes, dear."

"Of course a mother can tell, and I can tell you haven't been eating enough beef. Oh, we'll fix that. Won't we, Peter?" He nodded but she didn't wait for a reply. Every word was part of her mother's monologue. Charlotte was invited to listen but not to participate. She had long ago learned well enough that the best line of defense against the next tirade was to say nothing; anything else could be misconstrued.

"Look at you so skinny. No man will want you without some meat on your bones. Don't you want to get married? Have kids? You know there's a nice young man who's just moved next door. I've invited him over for dinner."

"Edith, dear, don't you think you should let Charlotte find her own men?" her father piped up to show his daughter he was on her side. He'd gotten a cart and was pushing her carry-on and her backpack; it was taking him all of his effort. She could have carried them more easily, but he was her father—he would carry her bags. This she understood, the same way she understood her mother's need to match her up again.

She was 47, and it wasn't that she hadn't wanted a husband and children—she really did—but she'd never found the right man. He wasn't in Hawaii, or New Zealand, or Thailand. Sometimes she wondered whether, if she had, would she then have been able to settle? Would she have been able to stop traveling? It wouldn't be fair to drag children around the world, she reasoned. Kids needed stability and routine. She needed freedom.

She knew by the time they reached the Caddy her parents had owned for 15 years that this trip had been a mistake, a futile respite from her loneliness in Costa Rica. She was tired of being alone, tired of having to cope with everything that came up, tired of never being able to depend on anyone else. But then, she should be used to being alone. It wasn't like she had ever really belonged with anyone.

All those years in school she'd sat back and watched the other kids. She wasn't a joiner. She just waited, marking time while watching the world. Twelve years to graduate, then she'd be free. Young Charlotte dreamed of all the places she would go. Now she'd been to all of them. There was nowhere left that she hadn't been—but she hadn't found what she'd sought in all these years and journeys. She didn't even know what it was. Perhaps there was no home, perhaps everyone was as homeless as she felt, just as disconnected from humanity as she was. Not being in their skins, she didn't know.

She looked up to see the stars, but there were none; the sky was filled with the orange haze of night, a glow against low clouds. Maybe later it would rain. She closed her eyes and thought of the nights in Costa Rica, the nights that had kept her there so long. In the encompassing darkness, with only the lights of distant galaxies, she would lie out on her hammock and watch the stars, and feel the beauty embrace her.

The freeway was as bland as always. She could never tell, the first day back in LA, which direction she was headed; it all felt the same. A light rain started falling, and the lights of the stores and houses were glowing like angels through the liquid diamonds on the windows. Her mother was still going on, selfish in her caring. "I'll make you a good meatloaf, yes, and when that boy comes over tomorrow night you be nice to him. He's losing his hair, but he's a lawyer, you know..." Charlotte automatically slipped into the mental fantasy of escape; she'd be leaving again—it didn't matter to where, as long as she was leaving.

The black SUV couldn't be seen as it approached their car. It was out of control, careening through the median barrier and slashing backwards through the rear door next to her, cleaving the Caddy in two before its passengers were crushed by the two halves as they rolled across the lanes of scattering traffic.

"Hello, can you hear me?" She woke up slowly, her entire body aching with the pain of immobility and disuse. The man looking at her was clad in a lab coat. She closed her eyes and tried to reopen them. What had happened...? Oh, the accident. She looked up at him. His yellow eyes gazed down at her. She shook her head and looked out around the room. Hundreds of bodies were hanging in stasis tubes. They weren't dead; she knew that, because she now remembered where she was. "It's always a little disorientating. How do you feel, ma'am? How was your trip?"

The seven fingers on his hand quickly administered a shot in her arm. Yes, she knew exactly where she was. She was home, and as she looked up into his five yellow eyes, she knew she'd been away too long. But she knew that she could never go home again. Shutting her yellow eyes, she started planning the next trip.

Chapter Ten

Tsunami

Louise looked over at the clock on the dash. She was late. It wasn't surprising, really. Michelle wouldn't be on time anyway; she never was. That was the excuse, the justification for being late. Louise would blame the traffic, say she'd got lost, and all of this was true. But still she didn't need to be late. If she'd just been able to walk away from her email and social media ten minutes earlier, she'd have been on time. Well, maybe, if she'd been able to also get Tanya away from that rerun of Tom and Jerry. They'd left the house the minute that was over. Louise had yelled the whole way, "Jump in the car, Justine,"—her oldest, with the googled directions in her hand. The directions said it would take fifteen minutes to get there but they were still on Sunset without even making the turn to go up into the Hollywood Hills and it had already been twenty.

"Mom, you have to turn left on North Gardner."

"Right, you mean?"

"Yeah, right." Louise tried to smile at her navigator; the ten-year-old needed all the encouragement she could get. Justine had inherited her inability to tell left from right from her mother, along with her brown hair, her crooked little toe, and her dyslexia. Louise understood exactly how hard life was for Justine. She wanted to be able to read, and do math, and know left from right, but more often she would transpose the two. Louise wanted her daughter to understand how smart and brilliant she was, but she knew Justine felt like a failure and struggled to keep up with her schoolwork. She hadn't wanted to come with her tonight. Justine had a math test tomorrow and she had asked to just stay home and study, but Louise had made her come. Although when Louise was ten kids had stayed home alone, she was a modern mother, and they didn't let their kids out of sight.

At the next road Louise turned right, then left on Hollywood Boulevard, but it wasn't until the next right that they left the world they knew behind. Behind them was the apartment they usually visited Michelle at, Michelle's home for the last twelve years, a large two-bedroom apartment on Fountain Boulevard built in the days before central air, when aluminum window frames were considered a luxury. Now the two-story rent-controlled stucco box was hot in the summer, with windows that wouldn't open—or if they did, wouldn't shut.

Michelle wasn't home, rather had invited Louise to bring the girls and their swimsuits to the place she was house-sitting at. Although only a few miles from the Westside apartment, it was obviously a step up, both physically and economically. They started to climb up into the Hills.

Los Angeles had always struck Louise as strange. When she'd moved here at twenty she hadn't understood how one street could be prestigious while the one two blocks down was too dangerous to walk at night. It made no sense that from one block to the next the wealth of the inhabitants could change by multiples of 10 or 100 or more.

The tree-lined street shaded the car and Louise willed her tension to fade. It wasn't her kids' fault she was going to be late. She regretted throwing Tanya into the car so roughly. At six, Tanya was the last kid in her class still needing a full car seat because she was too small for a booster. Louise tried to calm herself and her breathing. She put the Disney playlist on to mollify and apologize to her youngest and she knew she'd be forgiven when she heard Tanya start singing along to Hakuna Matata. She'd be there soon; there was no need to panic. Most of the houses were not visible from the street; only their gates were. Huge automatic gates and tall walls, the hallmarks of the oh-so-rich, or famous.

She kept climbing up the road. With all the green around her it was difficult to remember that she was in a desert in one of the worst droughts in history. She wondered momentarily how much water the average house in the hills wasted growing grass no one walked on. If the fires in nearby brown and blackened Griffith Park hadn't affected this world, nothing could. It was removed from the rest of the city, an enclave of wealth too rich to be affected by the disasters of the world. The road wound around in Jaimica Drive, a name reminiscent of the women who worked in the house cleaning and cooking, but not of any of the citizens of this kingdom. Then, if Jaimica Drive was not exclusive enough, they turned left (Justine got it right this time) into Jaimica Place.

There was only one house on the Place. It stood at the end of the road. A modern concrete and glass castle obviously built during the crazy building boom of the last few years. It had a gate, but the house towered over it, a series of glass and metal boxes reaching up into the sky. Louise wondered how many men it took to keep the glass clean as she drove up to the gate.

Pushing the button, she yelled into the box, "Hi, it's Louise." The gates slid away and she pulled up in front of one of the five garages. She hoped the car wasn't dripping oil; it would be a shame to leave a stain on the perfect slate surface of the driveway.

She walked to the back and opened the door for Tanya. Getting her out of the car was faster in the days when she was a baby strapped to a car seat. Now it seemed to take an age asking Tanya again and again to get out, watching her as she slowly found whatever shoes she had been wearing when she entered the car. Then, just when you thought she was ready to depart, she would start collecting up all her items for her purse, her strawberry lip gloss, her hair clips, her teddy bear. Then, slowly, she shoved them all in. Although six, Tanya was already a diva and would come when she was ready, and not before. Justine had already jumped out of the car and was approaching the house alone. The door opened for her, and Anabel threw her arms around Justine.

The two girls had known each other most of their lives. Two years Justine's junior, Anabel loved Justine and Justine wished Anabel would fall into a bottomless pit. Knowing the younger girl well, I understood Justine's exasperation. Finally, Tanya was ready and, purse in hand, she joined me so we could approach the door together.

"You have to see this house," crowed Anabel. "It's like so cool, and it's ours. Well, at least for now. One day I'll live in a house just like this. Mom said to take you up to the roof; we're having a barbeque."

A barbeque. Louise couldn't really imagine what that might hold when Michelle didn't cook or eat meat, but it sounded fun. A barbeque on the roof.

They stepped into a glass elevator hidden behind what looked like a regular door out of the entranceway. Then upward they went, slowly so they could see the view, slow enough that Louise found herself grasping the metal wall behind her as the girls stood noses to the glass. "That's our old apartment down there," said Anabel as if she would never have to go back to living on the flat land again.

The elevator door opened behind them and Louise fell backwards out onto the roof. The whole roof was a patio, with an infinity pool swimming towards the sunset, and blistering white furniture and ground. Michelle ran to her and hugged her in that very LA way, with air kisses over her shoulders. "Hey, Louise. Cool view, huh?"

Louise nodded, enjoying it more as she stepped away from the edges.

"I'll give you the grand tour after dinner," said Michelle, heading back to the grill. "It's all just about ready, and you don't want to miss the sunset from here."

"It sure is amazing. Any chance your client will be gone longer?"

"Nope. She rang to say she'll be back for sure in two weeks."

Michelle's client was a TV star, the kind that everyone recognizes and knows the name of. Michelle was her acupuncturist, and when she'd said she was leaving town for September, the hottest month of the year, Michelle had been quick to offer to housesit. The maid was on vacation and the house, all 7,000 square feet and four stories, was theirs for another two weeks.

"Where's Davis?"

"He had a client. I hope he'll be home by sunset." It was Friday. This was Michelle's tradition—family dinner, she called it—prayers, candles, food and friends. Louise and her kids often attended. On those occasions Michelle's husband Davis didn't come, you could see the disappointment and hurt in her eyes. Of course, she said nothing. She never complained; not about him, not about anything or anyone. Not even about Louise always being late.

"Mom."

Both women turned at the call but it was one of hers, so Louise walked over. Justine was standing on the edge of the roof, against the railing, arms crossed. "What's up, honey?"

"Anabel just offered to show me her new American Doll but told Tanya she couldn't see it because she'd make it dirty."

Louise rolled her eyes. Anabel was a horrid little brat, but then if she was being honest about her own daughter, Justine was a tattle-tale who never failed to complain. "I wanted to go play with Davina but I don't know where she is."

Davina was Michelle's three-year-old. She'd gone from being a sweet baby to being a demanding shrew in the last few months, but Justine still liked her company more than Anabel's. This may have been because Davina worshiped the ground Justine walked on, and Justine enjoyed being worshiped.

"Hey, Michelle, where's Davina?" Louise yelled.

"In the living room watching *Mermaidia* on the big screen. Have Anabel show you where." Michelle's head disappeared beneath the huge hood of the grill and Louise realized she was getting hungry.

"Anabel can you show Jessica and me around."

"She's just downstairs."

"It's a big house," sighed Louise, grabbing Tanya's hand. If she was going to have to go back in that elevator she needed all the emotional support she could get.

Michelle leaned around the grill. "Take them, Anabel. Then get up here quick. Food's just about ready."

Anabel led them into the glass elevator and Louise closed her eyes. One floor down they exited into a leather and steel living room. Louise stepped off the elevator and felt the ground shift under her feet. Climbing up the hills and that elevator must have upset her equilibrium. She hated heights. Davina lay on the animal skin rug just inches away from the 26-foot screen, looking up. The computer-animated Barbie looked even more disjointed and robotic than she normally did.

"Hey, Davina," Louise yelled, but Davina didn't hear her. Justine walked over to her and swung her up into her arms.

"Oh, Da-Da-Davina," she said in a baby voice. "Come on, dinner's ready." Justine brought Davina to the elevator, and they shut the door to the house behind them. The shiny metal and modern art statues made her feel uneasy and Louise had no desire to enter, least she leave behind footprints. She wondered how long it was going to take Michelle to scrub and clean the house clean enough for the maid.

Arriving back on the roof deck the girls ran towards the table where Michelle had laid out snacks. Louise followed them slowly, feeling a rolling under her feet and a lack of balance.

"Is there anything I can do?"

"Sure. Bring plates over here and I'll start serving."

Louise was taking the plates to the table when she noticed the view had changed. That was LA, that was Century City, that was Santa Monica... but the ocean looked wrong, too brown. When they turned on the news later they'd probably hear someone had just broken a tanker full of oil into the sea, or there was some huge sewage spill again. God help the seals. She went back to Michelle.

"Look," she said, pointing. They stared together, and the children joined them on the edge of the deck while behind them the vege hot dogs shriveled on the fire.

The brown was spreading outward, towards Catalina. And now it was blue again, but a strange blue. They couldn't see Catalina. The sky—no, the sea—had eaten it, devoured the barrier islands, and on the sea surged. In a moment that took a hundred years they held their breaths and the sea charged forward. The wave looked small from where they were, just like the 30-story buildings looked small. And then the sky-scrapers were gone, and so was Santa Monica.

"Mommy." Justine clutched Louise's waist and Louise pulled Tanya into her, but their eyes never left the ocean. Out it surged again, all the water in the world pulling back, forming another assault. And in it rushed. They couldn't see the city, they couldn't see land at all for water. They were on an island now, and around them was nothing.

"Davis," Michelle whimpered from the back of her throat. Davina was in her arms playing with her hair while Anabel stood alone, her face white, her mouth screaming nothing, silent tears pouring down her face. Michelle ran to her, and Anabel started to hit her, lashing out at the only person she could.

The water didn't recede this time but stayed. The next earthquake they all felt, it was closer and they could see the water rising.

Michelle tried calling Davis but there was no signal. There was no electricity to power the 24-foot TV or stereo system so they just waited.

The night fell over the submerged city with a darkness the children had never experienced. And then the moon rose large, so large over the ocean. And Louise knew it was an optical illusion, that the moon could not be that big, and then the moon rose higher in the sky and Louise understood the earthquake wasn't something that had happened to Los Angeles. The moon was closer than it had ever been. This wasn't the shifting of one tectonic plate, this was the rippling of the earth in response to its satellite changing orbit.

Louise hadn't thought anything about the mining work they were starting on the moon, but now, with the angry face of the moon looking down on her, she knew that man's greed had caused this, that somehow the mining project had shifted the orbit.

Michelle looked up at the moon and pointed. She'd noticed it to. Both her children were in her arms where they had collapsed when they realized their father was dead. Michelle said nothing and just pointed with a confused look.

Louise didn't want to explain it. If she was right it was too horrible. Too terrifying and sad.

They'd eaten the burnt vege dogs for breakfast by the time the submarine came to take them off the roof. They huddled in with the other survivors—famous celebrities, millionaires and their maids and gardeners with bandanas tied around their necks. The only people high up enough to survive.

Louise walked down into the metal box and thought for a moment. What now? Where do we go? She tried not to think. The door slammed down and she held her daughters to her. When the next quake hit they were in the ocean over Culver City. As the submarine rolled over, Louise held her daughters even tighter and screamed.

Pride

Chapter Eleven

AlOne

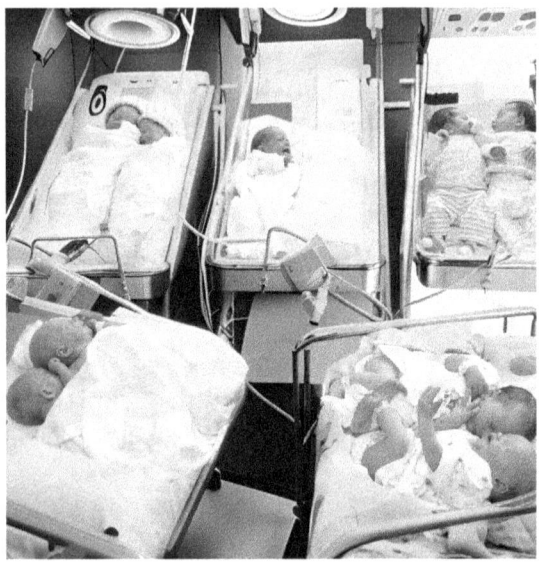

"Terri and Sherri, have you met Una? Una, this is Sherri and Terri." I had to wonder why parents insisted on calling twins by rhyming names. Surely when you had identical twins it was hard enough to tell them apart without giving them similar names.

"Hello. Nice to meet you." Two more names I was supposed to memorize, supposed to know, but I would forget as soon as I walked away. I always did. Then the next time we were at some social event together they would call me, and I would stand there making small talk without using their name, pretending I remembered it, pretending I remembered them.

Catherine was only trying to help. She was my best friend. She had always been my best friend, her and Anne. People always remembered my name, remembered my face. They would have heard about me before I even arrived at the party. When I walked in all eyes had been on me; they'd known who I was even before I knew their names. Right now they were just waiting for me to turn around and leave so they could discuss the freak.

Sherri stared at me, looking for the defect. Terri's eyes were turned to the floor, either in fear or because she had better manners. I started trying to work out which it was. Fear, I decided. Sherri was the dominant twin and Terri was the subordinate. Sherri would tell her what to think of me later.

Anne came over and took my hand. "Excuse me, ladies, Catherine, but I need Una for a moment." I turned and smiled at Anne. I'd always been able to tell them apart, even when they were young. Catherine and Anne had never tried to look alike. They'd never tried to fool me like the other twins in my class. Anne always wore pink, Catherine always wore red. Anne's hair was always long, Catherine's always short. I had never understood why most twins wanted to look alike. Wasn't it enough to see your own face when you turned around? What was it, some kind of extreme narcissism?

I could hear them talk about me as I turned.

"She looks sort of normal; you wouldn't know."

"There's no way she's well socialized."

"Poor thing. I mean, she's never going to be able to marry now, is she?"

No, of course I couldn't marry or have any kind of life at all. I mean, I am one.

Catherine leaned in and whispered in my ear, "Just ignore them. They're idiots too stupid to know you aren't even out of earshot yet. Come on. Mike and John are out running the grill. Let's go get something to eat." It was better than being inside with the shrews. At least the men outside wouldn't care if I was a freak; they'd be too busy checking out my legs, and Mike and John were nice enough.

The wedding would be in June. Anne and Catherine had both picked me as their maid of honor; it was untraditional only having one. I couldn't really tell the difference between Mike and John; they seemed so alike, so generic—not nearly good enough for Anne and Catherine, but maybe they each found something unique in their partner, or perhaps they liked to change it up, one one night and one the other. I didn't like to ask. I didn't really know how it worked in a normal household, a household with two couples, a normal twin/twin marriage. How was I supposed to know? I didn't grow up in a normal household—my arrival had destroyed any normality my parents may have had.

"Burger, or a hot dog?" asked Mike/John or John/Mike. Maybe one of them could grow a beard, or a little pointy waxed moustache.

I started to laugh at the image of this clean-cut young man twirling the end of his pointy moustache and just managed to blurt out hot dog. He handed it over quick enough and I went to sit under the tree. Catherine and Anne joined me.

"How are your parents doing? It's been a while since I've seen them." Anne really wanted to know. They'd grown up next door, in our house most of the time. I think they loved my mother at least as much as I did, and I was sure that my mother probably loved them more than she loved me.

"She wants to move into a nursing home."

Catherine almost coughed out the lettuce she was chewing on. She was already stick thin, but she wanted to stay that way until after the wedding. "What do you mean, nursing home? She's not that old and she's not sick, is she?"

"No, just lonely in that big house and wants to be around people." They looked down at their food and said nothing. They understood.

My parents had moved into our house with high hopes. It was a standard double house—two master bedrooms, four other bedrooms, one large living room, 6 bathrooms and two kitchens. My dad and my mother were the first ones to conceive. While my aunt and uncle were still working on their careers and saving money to decorate their side of the house, my mom got pregnant on or before the wedding. From the beginning it wasn't a normal pregnancy. Don't believe the rumors; I was never a twin, there was never another me, I didn't kill my twin in utero, and she didn't die at birth. It was just me, and one day, weeks before they thought I should come, I shot out into the world alone.

The doctors couldn't put me back or fix it, so they did what they could. They tested me. It was a genetic error, a recessive gene so rare that the odds of my parents both having it were one billion to one. I was the one billion. My aunt and uncle, of course, both had the gene too and decided at that moment never to conceive. I heard for a while they tried to adopt but no adoption agency was willing to put other children in the same house as me.

I wasn't supposed to live. Singles hadn't lived before. People could not survive alone; everyone knew that. When my grandaunt had gotten sick my grandmother got sick and they both died on the same day. That's always the best way. My granddad had to go get euthanized when his brother had his heart attack. I remembered their funerals, social occasions for family, and me sitting in the corner trying not to be noticed.

"Could you please do something about the way your men dress?" I asked, trying to change the subject. "They look so damn alike, and I can't tell them apart."

"They look the same naked too," laughed Catherine.

"Ok, too much detail. Just color-code them for me or something. You know, like you guys always wear pink and red."

"But they want to look the same."

"Tell you what, just for you, we'll buy them different belts. John black, Mike brown."

"But they'll probably swap. They like wearing each other's clothes," Catherine said looking her man—or was it Anne's man—up and down appreciatively.

"Have you been out lately?"

"No." It wasn't like I hadn't tried. I'd been on a few dates with twins whose twin had died, the ones without enough courage to die immediately, but it always seemed like they were dying anyway, just slowly, and my last long-term relationship had been with one of them. It had taken him 3 months to get the same kind of cancer his brother had died of, and 6 months to die of it. I'd advertised for the third in a triplet set, hoping there was one where they'd gotten together with a twin set and there was an odd man out, but triplets were even closer than twins and they only wanted to be with triplets. Besides, I could never have children, so what was I really good for anyway?

"You know, you should keep trying. There's someone for everyone."

"I think I'm just meant to be alone." I looked down at my feet. I didn't want to discuss this, I didn't want to make my friends sad, I didn't want to spend my time with them berating my own single existence. Soon they would be gone, sucked into the happy void of marriage, and I would have lost them too. The time we had was precious, too precious to waste. "I'm applying for a new job."

"Oh, that's great," they said in unison. They did that a lot, that and finishing each other's sentences. They didn't think about it; it was what everyone did, everyone but me.

"Yeah, it's kind of a surprise but I go for the interview tomorrow and I'll let you know how it goes."

******

"Hello. Please sit down." He had heavy glasses, but they were in his hand, not on his face—vain enough not to wear them when we met, blind enough not to put them down where he couldn't find them. I'd seen his twin in the elevator. They probably worked in the same department, maybe even shared the same job. That was the reason I couldn't get most jobs; I just couldn't fit in. My degree in biology meant nothing, my master's in genetics nothing. I'd done it to amuse myself. I'd toyed with the idea of going for a PhD—why not; I enjoyed school much more than I enjoyed my job as a waitress.

I sat obediently in front of him. I handed my resume over and he put it down on the desk without looking at it. He was staring at me instead, trying to focus his small eyes. "Good." He nodded, his combover shifting on his slick head. "Now let me tell you about the position. We are looking for someone who is willing to go to our space station and live there for six months before returning. You would be doing gene research, and DNA splicing."

"That sounds fantastic."

"There's only one catch, you see. You'd have to go alone. With the weight of the equipment you need to take, we don't have a vessel that will get you two and the gear out of earth's orbit. You'd have to leave your twin behind. I know it's an unreasonable request, but the government has cut our budget so much... That, and the space station only has enough supplies for three months if we send both you and your sister, and the tests really will take six months to complete."

"I don't have a sister."

"Oh, I am so sorry." He started to put his glasses on and look down at her resume. "When did she die? How much longer do you have?"

"I never had a sister."

He slid his glasses on properly and stared down at my resume. "You are Una."

"Yes."

"I have heard of you. I was going to tell you we have installed video conferencing so you won't be too alone but... you won't need that, will you?"

"It would be nice to talk to my friends and family."

"Of course, you have parents. How rude of me." He read to the bottom of my resume in complete silence and then he looked me up and down.

"You may be the only person on earth qualified for this job."

"Yes, I probably am."

"Why would you want to go alone into space?"

"Because it would be easier than being alone in a crowd. Will you hire me?"

"Yes," he said.

I smiled the smile of one freed from her cage.

Chapter Twelve

Jacob's Ladder Down

J acob Levin was working late again. The room was dark, except for the light above his drafting table. The comfortable chair where he could put on a mind-cap and interface with the computer was barely visible in the shadows. The cleaning crew had already finished, and the night-time office shift had not yet begun.

Jacob, a Traditionalist, rarely used the mind-cap, instead using a pen and paper. The pen, a ballpoint he had acquired at an antique auction, still worked well—although he had to make the ink to refill its plastic reservoir. The drafting table was an antique, too. There had always been a designer or engineer in his family and the table had been handed down to him from Great-Grandfather David—exactly how many greats ago no one could remember. He rubbed his hands down the dented wooden legs. When he was a small child, he always measured himself against the drafting table. He had known that as soon as he was as tall as the back of the table, he would be a man.

Jacob yawned and pushed his glasses up his nose. Resting his head on his hand, he looked down at his design. It was almost finished. The last brace was on the wrong angle. He picked up the laser wand and disintegrated the ink particles that comprised the error, and made his correction.

Done. He could see exactly how his device would work. Despite his two-dimensional medium, the builders always found his plans easy to follow. He thought through every detail, down to the actual nuts and bolts of a design. His latest effort would serve to control the rodent population of one of Earth's new space colonies. It would also yield a natural soil amendment for agricultural terraforming of the planet.

Jacob pushed himself out of his chair and walked to the elevator. "Floor 1003B," he said. It slid effortlessly to his part of the building. He had only a couple of seconds to worry about what Beth would say. He could hear her voice already, as he had heard it so many times before, higher than normal, loud and sharp, accusing.

"You're late again. Had to keep working, I suppose! I made dinner but it's burnt."

He had tried once, when they had only been married a few months, to argue with her. "You don't have to cook. Just buy meals at the market like everyone else." She had looked at him as though he were a complete stranger.

"Jacob Levin! I married you because you were a Traditionalist. We agreed to eat only proper Kosher food, proper vegetables and meat, not some meal thrown together in a factory by a machine. I spent two hours at the market today fighting 400,000 other people who were also shopping, because I wanted to make you a nice meal—and you don't even show up." She had started to cry, and he'd wrapped his arms around her.

"I'm sorry, honey. I really am. It won't happen again." But it had, again and again. He just got caught up in the beauty of the machines he was creating and forgot everything else. Even the woman he had once said he would love forever.

The beeping light was telling him to leave the elevator, but he did so reluctantly. The corridor was crowded, as usual. Twenty million people lived and worked in his building, and bodies jostled him, but he didn't feel them. Most people rode the walk paths, but he considered that lazy. It was almost midnight. Beth would be angry.

"Flowers for your lover, sir?" A peddler pushed roses under Jacob's nose; replicated roses, of course—the real thing was impossibly expensive. "You look like you might need them, coming home so late and all."

The peddler pointed to Jacob's white jumpsuit with the insignia that said he was a government design engineer. The white jumpsuit marked him as a day worker, a professional man. The peddler, an old man with a scar across his left cheek, pushed the roses into his face again but he ignored them as he had learnt to do and kept walking. Flowers would not appease Beth; fifteen years of marriage had taught him that much. She would never leave him, but she would also never forgive him.

He put his right hand on the scanner and his front door opened. He walked in and sighed with relief. She was asleep on the sofa. Her soft, black hair fell across her face, her mouth was open, velvet lips almost smiling. No wrinkles or worry lined her face. It was still the face of the young girl he had married so long ago. Her black eyes, now closed, would be filled with deep disappointment tomorrow.

The table was laid perfectly with three plates and two candles. Their son's food had been eaten but Beth's and his own were untouched. It was his favorite meal, stew and challah bread, but he didn't want it now. He looked in on Samuel, who was sound asleep in his bed. They needed to take a vacation after he finished this design. He had to spend time with this family. Every time someone asked him how old his son was he would always answer "Five," but then would have to correct himself with "Sorry—ten." He walked into the room and pulled the covers up to his son's chin, and tucked them in. Samuel had always slept restlessly, fighting to leave his childhood. Jacob kissed him gently on the forehead and went back to Beth.

She had turned and was lying on her back, her hands beautifully arranged on her chest. He picked her up gently and carried her to bed. She curled against him. "Jacob," she murmured, her voice deep with sleep, in love with him still—when she wasn't awake.

He lay in bed still thinking of his design. The new planet was covered in large biped rodents and had an oxygen-based atmosphere. It could be settled immediately—at least as soon as the rodent population issue was cured. The animals apparently subsisted on the soil and depleted the natural fertility of the planet. Tests had proved that modified Earth crops would grow there in abundance, except that the rodents kept destroying the crops. His machine would not only exterminate the vermin but would work so efficiently that the organic material of their bodies could be used for fertilizer. The machine, when it was constructed, would use no poisons or other toxins. There would be no waste that had to be disposed of later; it was totally environmentally friendly. He had worried about how the animals would be made to enter the machine, but he was told they were easily herded.

He set the alarm clock and left for work early, before Beth had awoken. He had scarcely slept and when he did, all he dreamed of was his machine. Back at the drafting table, he went over the whole design again. At midday he scanned it into the network so his supervisor could review it.

He waited anxiously, sure that his design was good. Nevertheless, the longer he waited the more he was sure that he had forgotten something, that he had failed. He watched the computer screen, waiting for a response.

"The design is perfect. You are to go to the point of installation and ensure that it is functioning as quickly as possible. For matters of convenience, your family will accompany you. Please report back to your housing unit and wait for Transportation to contact you."

He read the computer screen twice. The point of the installation—that meant leaving the Earth. Jacob had never left the building he was born in, let alone the planet. The building, after all, was complete for all his needs. He had seldom seen Outside. All the rooms with windows were occupied by the extremely wealthy. He had been to Central Park on Level 1-2N when he was younger, on vacation. It had been cold, and he had gotten sick.

He would be outside on an uninhabited planet. Fear and excitement grabbed him. He printed out the order, grabbed his pen, the plans, and patted the desk affectionately. He longed to tell someone, but they were all deep inside their computers and he never spoke to them anyway.

He ran to the elevator and traveled the familiar path back home. Beth would probably be cleaning. Being a Traditionalist, she didn't work, so there was no need to worry about her getting time off. Samuel's school would let him have the time off—how often does a boy get such an educational opportunity?

The short hike to the apartment seemed to take forever. He ran in the corridors, trying not to push and shove. His right hand hit the sensor while his left hand pushed the door open.

"Beth, Beth."She came into the room slowly. In his excitement he didn't see the dried tears on her cheeks. "What are you doing home, Jacob?" she said slowly, accusing, trying to get angry.

"Beth, look at this." He handed her the order.

"What does this mean?"

"We are going off-planet. They want me to supervise the installation of my newest machine design."

She felt her stomach sink as fear of the unknown filled her. Yet, it was a chance for her to spend some time with the man she seemed to have lost somewhere between "I love you" and "I'm late for work."

"I will call Samuel's school. You start packing. We have to be at Transportation by midnight. It's a thirty-minute ride on the walk path."

Samuel ran home, happy in the way that a schoolboy with time off school is. He ran into his parents' room. "What are you going there for, Dad?"

"To kill rodents."

"Rodents? You mean like pests; rats or mice?"

"Yes.""Ugh, gross."

"Samuel, go get your suitcase. I've packed all your clothes; we do not know what the climate will be like."

"Climate?" Beth just scowled at him, and he went to get the suitcase.

Jacob wondered what climate changes were like. Having always lived inside the building, he had never given it much thought. The weather was always the same, the temperature always right, and the lighting was always appropriate. If you worked nights, the light hours were during the night, and if you worked days, the light hours were during the day. Of course, working during the day had more prestige, but for all practical purposes it made no difference.

Beth was still angry at him. He wanted to ask her forgiveness for all his mistakes, to tell her he would never disappoint her again. But this was not the time. They were packed. It was better to move. There was no reason to stay. Beth's sister would come and clean out the refrigerator for them tomorrow. She would look after their place until they got back. Their home seemed abandoned already. He wondered how long it would be before he saw his wooden drafting table again.

They started on the walk path. Samuel was tired now; he leaned against Jacob.

"Mommy, I want to lie down."

"No, Samuel. The walk path is filthy. We'll be there soon enough." She reached out to him and brushed his hair back off his face.

On arrival at Transport, Jacob presented the travel order.

"Yes, Mr. Levin, you are on the list. Please proceed through the main doors, turn right and take the corridor to Gate 243," said the young, uniformed official looking at his computer screen.

Having never been wealthy enough to travel, Jacob had never been to Transport before. He found, much to his disappointment, that once through Transport's main doors the corridors looked exactly the same as the other ones in the building, except most of the people were carrying luggage. Samuel's eyes were closing so Jacob lifted him up and laid him on top of the suitcases, where he fell asleep instantly. They arrived at Gate 243 in half an hour and Jacob, who had thought he was being taken to the space vessel, was surprised to find that Gate 243 was only a waiting room for inter-building shuttles. Apparently, the space vessel was going to depart from the roof of another building. Beth's face registered his own shock that another building was in some way superior to their own, for they'd always been told their building was the best.

Jacob pushed their cart into the shuttle. Beth, who was not talking to him, strapped herself into the chair while he secured the luggage and placed Samuel in a chair, buckling him in. The shuttle went sideways, then waited for clearance. It took off forward and they were pushed into the seats by the acceleration force. The other people on the shuttle seemed to think it was all a matter of course; they were obviously seasoned travelers. Jacob found himself pleasantly surprised to find Beth's hand gripping his knee as the shuttle accelerated. He hoped the actual space vessel would be easier on her. Samuel remained asleep, as only exhausted children can.

Jacob watched through the window. He wanted to see the Outside. When at last they cleared the building, the window was covered in water, the Outside dark. Jacob thought for a moment, then realized this must be rain. How very disappointing and odd, he thought. He looked at Beth. Her face, too, was angled toward the window and tears were rolling down her cheeks, like the rain outside. "What's wrong, honey?"

She flicked her tears away. "I'm not really sure. I'm just scared, I suppose."

He thought about it for a moment and could instantly feel the fear that was hidden under his excitement—fear of the unknown, a sense of loss at leaving the familiar. "It is going to be all right, Beth. It will be a whole new start for us." She smiled up at him, wanting to believe him. The rain stopped hitting the window and they were glad, for it meant that they had entered another building, a more familiar environment. The shuttle came in quickly and stopped with a jolt, waking even Samuel.

"Are we there yet?"

"No, darling," Beth said, sweeping his glossy black hair back from his eyes. "We are in the place where we will catch the space vessel."

"Oh, cool," he said, instantly awake. "Where is the one we are going on?" There was nothing but the white walls to be seen from the window.

"Your name and destination." Jacob answered the official's question quickly and asked where their space vessel was.

"Take walk path 4B. It will take you directly to your vessel. You will be departing in 20 minutes."

Twenty minutes! Suddenly everything seemed to be going too fast. The walk path took them there quickly and they saw the space vessel for the first time. It was large, as large as a building it seemed, and white.

"Wow," said Samuel. Beth and Jacob could think of nothing to say as the walk path led them right up to the loading door of the vessel, which seemed to grow more impossibly large as they neared it.

"Jacob Levin, wife and child?" Jacob nodded at the uniformed woman standing at the door. "This way, sir. Please follow me to your berthing. Take off will be in 16 minutes."

Samuel bounced along, taking everything in, while Jacob, totally overwhelmed, tried to focus on the floor. He looked over at Beth and saw she was doing the same thing. They were soon in their room, which was large by their standards. There were two beds—a double one for them and a single for Samuel—set against the rear wall.

"Make yourselves comfortable. You will find a food replication unit against the starboard wall for any food or refreshments," the woman said, pointing.

"How long will it take for us to get there?" Beth asked, and Jacob felt stupid for not having asked earlier.

"You will be there in three days. I am sure you will find your journey pleasant. We have a large video library, as well as a recreation room and a bar in the aft. There is a complete map and guide to shipboard services on your bedside table." The woman turned and left them before they could ask any more questions.

The next three days were the only vacation Jacob Levin had ever taken with his family. They found that takeoff was simple, rather easier, in fact, than the shuttle had been, due to the ship's artificial gravity. By the second day even Beth had relaxed enough to eat the shipboard food without a murmur. The vessel was lavish; space travel was one of the most profitable businesses ever, yet it was becoming increasingly difficult to recruit crew. Most people were just too afraid of the unknown to risk their lives in space. In order to attract more recruits, the vessels were becoming larger and larger, with better living spaces for the crew and the occasional passengers.

Samuel ran around the ship, adapting to the new life. He even went to the bridge to look out into space at the path ahead of them. Jacob wanted to go see their equipment, but in truth there was a fear that somehow looking at the stars would cause him to be swallowed up by the blackness.

When they heard they had finally reached their location, Beth and Jacob were led by Samuel up to the observation deck. It was daytime and the world below twinkled green and blue the way it was said that Earth once looked. The enormity of it somehow helped Jacob, who did not believe his eyes. It was a beautiful picture, like others he had seen of planets, but it didn't register as being real. He found himself thinking about the project again. The holiday was over—it was time to kill some rodents.

While Beth organized their luggage for leaving the ship Jacob went through the plans again. He wondered what the rodents of the planet looked like. What did it matter? His machine would deal with them soon enough. In a couple of weeks they could have it fully functioning. Then he would be sure to get a raise, perhaps be put in charge of his department. Maybe they could even get an apartment with a window, a small window, with a view Outside.

Samuel could go to a better school and learn engineering and design. Maybe he could one day be an intergalactic engineer, traveling the universe putting in his designs. Perhaps if this project went well Jacob would be able to install even more of his designs. He could show his family the universe, give them a life that few were able to experience. "We have landed. Jacob, Jacob..." He looked up from his daydream to see Beth standing in front of him. "Please push the luggage cart for me, Jacob. We are leaving."

It wasn't until the door opened that Jacob realized he had been holding his breath. The entranceway from the space dock to the building had been covered. They were still inside. The Outside was there, but they didn't have to face it, not yet.

A burly man, overfed, in a uniform that was too tight around the neck, greeted them. "Hello. I'm Commandant Johnstone. I am in charge of Base Administrations." He pointed to a thin woman with an unhealthy parlor. "This is my assistant Andrea. She will accompany you to your quarters."

"Thank you. I'm Jacob Levin—""Well, of course you are. Now settle in tonight. Tomorrow be at my office at 9 a.m. sharp." Commandant Johnstone turned before Jacob could respond and marched off down the causeway. Andrea picked up a bag and followed him in silence. Together, they followed her into the building.

Their apartment was beautiful and spacious. There were windows, but someone had thoughtfully installed both blinds and heavy drapes, and the only light came from the electrical fittings. "Make yourselves at home," said Andrea, as she put down the bag she had carried. "The refrigerator is full of food. We were told you ate a Kosher diet, so we placed a special order. The climate control is regulated, and you don't have to go outside or look out the windows. I never do, so it's almost like home."

Beth seemed to sag, like the terror was no longer holding her up and now she could relax. Jacob smiled; it would be ok. "Thank you, Andrea."

She nodded and left, closing the door behind her.

The commandant's office was huge. It would have housed thirty executives back home, and yet the commandant didn't look smaller behind his huge teak desk; he looked bigger. "So, Mr. Levine, we have seen your plans. We only have a few questions."

"Yes, sir."

"Electrical generation. We understand that this plant will require large amounts of electricity." The commandant seemed to be looking past him, at the wall behind.

"Yes, I studied this. Given the nature of the planet, with its annual precipitation and trade winds, I suggested a combination of hydro-electric and wind turbine generation. The hydro dam could also be used for irrigation purposes, and after the rodents were gone this power source could be redirected for use by the settlers." Jacob turned to look at what the commandant was looking at. There on the wall was a lion's head. Jacob was sure it was a lion's head; he'd seen one once in a museum. It must be priceless.

"Yes, very commendable ideas."

"The plan was approved before I left."

"Yes, but the time and money required for hydro-dam construction... Well, quite frankly, it's not within my budget. You have no idea how tight the budget is up here."

"I see." Jacob ran his hand over the edge of the desk. It was beautiful.

"Would you like a drink?" the commandant asked.

"No, thank you."

The commandant walked over to a wall cabinet and poured himself a glass of 100-year-old French brandy. He walked back, and before he sat in his leather chair he started again, "So, we need to reduce costs on your machine."

"Reduce costs..."

"Yes. The base obtains its electricity from a small fusion reactor and it seems this would be a logical way to power the plant."

"Sir, you're talking about a small magnetic containment reactor. The original energy needed to heat the plasma was provided at time of production and transported after the chain reaction had started, but that reactor wouldn't have the necessary output to heat the fuel of a new secondary reactor."

"Glad to hear you know what you're talking about, so just hop to it, ok?"

"Sir, it won't work."

"Mr. Levin, I was told you were the best. A great engineer. If you are not up for the task, then I'll just tell the Company. We can arrange a return ship to take you home next week."

Jacob felt the threat echo through him. He wanted to build his machine. He was proud of his work, he wanted to see the machine built, wanted for once to touch the cogs and wheels.

He looked around the office once more. A woven rug—it looked handmade and antique—the huge wooden desk in teak and mahogany made with mortise joints, the kind that few people had used in the last few centuries. The problem was obvious; the commandant had already spent the budget. There was no budget left for the machine. Jacob looked up at the commandant. The commandant sat on his leather seat relaxed and confident. Jacob knew he would not change the man or the situation. If Jacob wanted to build his machine, he would need to replace the electrical generation equipment.

"Unless, of course, you think you can build your machine to accommodate the budgetary constraints." The unveiled threat reminded Jacob that he would have to find a solution or go home a failure.

"I will try, sir."

"Of course. Present your new plans to me." The commandant dismissed him with a wave of the hand without ever looking at Jacob.

* * * * *

"Put that pen down and eat your food." Jacob looked up at Beth. When had she started treating him like a child? Before, he'd spent his days at the office. Now there was nowhere to work but at the apartment. He sat scribbling, trying to come up with a solution to the problem. They were alone together all day, every day. Samuel had taken only a few days to find his way Outside. He ran and played in the sun while Jacob and Beth stayed inside finding new ways to irritate each other. Too afraid to even open the curtains, neither of them planned to venture Out. Jacob just wanted to finish the plans and leave. His dream of a vacation with his family where everyone was happy had faded. Now he just wanted to endure, finish the project and go home, to his drafting table.

"Yes, Beth." He shoveled some food without tasting it. The budget was just so tight, there was no way to generate the power, unless...

Jacob pushed away from the table and put the mind-cap on to connect with the computer.

"Jacob!" Beth yelled, but he couldn't hear her; he was deep in the computer banks. Beth put down her fork and went into the bedroom to cry.

What was she doing here? Jacob barely spoke to her; Samuel didn't need her. No one needed her. Even the food she made was hardly eaten. She'd hoped the change of location would help, that if she could just spend more time with Jacob the holes in their marriage would mend. Now she felt she was falling into a chasm and Jacob was left standing above her. They couldn't be together even when they tried.

She dried her eyes and went back to the living room. He looked so relaxed, so young, so happy. He never looked like that with her anymore. She touched him gently on the shoulder, but he didn't notice. She put his food next to him and cleaned up the table. Where was Samuel? She wanted to go out and check on him, but she couldn't. She went to the window and pulled the drape. Light tried to peak through the slats of the blind. *Tomorrow, I'll pull the blinds up.* She knew even then that it was a lie. She sat down and plugged herself into the computer; at least that would pass the time.

There it was. It was old technology, no one used it anymore, but it would work, and he could do it within budget. All he needed was a volcano. He unplugged and looked around the room. Beth was plugged in. She looked so beautiful. Her eyes were closed but they were swollen; she'd been crying again.

Samuel came in, "Hi, Dad."

"Hi, Samuel. What have you been doing?"

Samuel shook his head. "Dad, you have no idea. You have to come see."

"Maybe after I get the plan finished." Then he would have to venture Outside to see them build his machine. Until then, well, he had work to do.

"I made a friend."

"A friend? I didn't think there were any other kids on the base."

"He doesn't live on the base. He's not a person."

Jacob nodded. Samuel had always had imaginary friends when he was young. The doctor had assured them it was normal; it made sense that he would have another one now that he was alone. "Great. What do you do together?"

"Just explore and stuff. There are cool caves and a lake."

"Be careful."

Jacob's watch phone rang, and he looked down to see who it was. The commandant. He ignored it.

"Shouldn't you take that?"

"I'll talk to him in a minute."

"Look, it's ok, Dad. There's a panic button on my phone. If there's any problems security will come get me."

"Ok," said Jacob. What else could he say? Stay inside with your mother and me while we tear each other's souls apart? He'd wanted his son to see the Outside, to have fun, to experience another life. He'd underestimated his own fear and overestimated his capacity to adjust. He'd thought he'd go Outside too.

Jacob's phone started to ring again—the commandant. There was knocking on the door. He hit the comm button on his phone and walked towards the door. He opened the door. Andrea was there.

"Yes," he said to the phone.

"We need to start construction. Where's your plans, engineer?" the commandant's voice bellowed from the earpiece in Jacob's ear.

"The commandant would like to see you," said Andrea.

"I'm on my way," he said to Andrea and the commandant simultaneously.

"So, where are your plans?" said the commandant without so much as a hello.

"Is there an active volcano on the planet?"

"Yes, several. What difference does that make? We need to start construction. How are we going to power this thing? You know they want to send the first settlers in a year? We need to clean up the rodent population now! That's all your job is, engineer—bug killer!" He stopped for air so Jacob took the opportunity.

"Low heat fusion."

"I told them sending one of you groundlings was a mistake. Have you ever even been outside? Has moving off planet made you completely insane.? Low heat fusion—I've never heard of it... What the hell is low heat fusion?""Fusion requires heat, extreme heat. Generating heat requires electricity. The current electrical plant is insufficient to power another plant larger than itself."

"Low heat fusion?"

"It was pioneered three centuries ago. The heat for the fusion chain reaction and the heating of the plasma is reduced by increasing the ambient external temperature."

"Huh?"

"If we build a magnetic containment fusion reactor that can be placed into a geothermal vent close to a source of magma and then utilized the heat of the magma" Jacob saw the commandant's eyes glaze over. "Normally it would take a lot of heat to start a fusion reaction, but if we use the magma—" the commandant still looked confused "—the molten lava to heat up the generator, then we can also generate some electricity through steam, we should be able to get the fusion reaction going. Low heat fusion can power the reactor."

"How much will it cost?"

"I can do it within your budget."

The commandant grabbed a drink. "What do you know, the engineer actually managed to do it! We started construction on the plant last week."

"But you said that—"

"I couldn't slow down the project that much, so how soon can you make this reactor?"

"I'll need men and materials."

"Send me the list. I want it done in two weeks."

* * * * *

"So today we went on a hike up a high mountain. You should have seen the view from up there! We could see Harry's village from up there, then Harry and I threw rocks down the slope towards this big river. Then we walked down to the river and Harry and I went swimming. Then he actually caught a fish in the river with his hands—with his hands! Can you imagine?"

"That's nice, Samuel," said Beth. She was pushing her food around her plate. Jacob watched her. She was getting thin, she'd stopped yelling, she scarcely spoke, she just answered when spoken to. He didn't even know how to reach her. He wanted to know what words he should say, what would fix everything.

"Who's Harry?"

"Samuel's friend, Jacob, you know—"

"Oh yes." Harry was the imaginary friend. Beth was frowning. He'd cut her off again. He hadn't meant to. What was he supposed to say now? "There is a whole village of Harrys?" asked Jacob.

"Oh yeah. There are tons of villages, all over the place."

"Great, great. How are you doing on your classes on the computer?"

"It's easy enough. I'll probably be ahead of the other kids by the time we go back. When are we going home, Dad?"

Beth looked at him as if this was the one thing he could do for her, that if nothing else, he could take her home. "I should be able to get the plant up and running in the next couple of weeks."

"Oh, do we have to? Can't we stay here? I mean it's so great—trees, and rivers and sun. You guys got to come out and see it. I mean, it's amazing."

"I am going out today to see the machine." He knew he had to go see the machine. It was ready to go. Everything except the reactor was in place. "Could you go with me, Samuel?" Maybe if Samuel held his hand, he'd be able to be brave. He wanted to see the machine, to see if it had turned out like it was in his head.

"Cool. Well, I'd better do my homework now." Samuel pushed himself away from the table and put on the mind-cap. Now Jacob and Beth were alone again, together, staring at each other across the table.

"The dinner was great, Beth. Thank you." She nodded.

"We need to talk." She looked up, her eyes large and scared. He started with the only thing he was sure she wanted to hear.

"I'm sorry."

"I can't do this anymore." She started to cry. He didn't know what to say next, so he just put his arms around her. She started to cry louder; he held her tight.

"I love you." That was it, all he had. If that wasn't enough, he didn't know what to do next. She kept weeping, pushing her face into his shirt, mucus running onto his clothes. He reached for a napkin and started to wipe her face. "It's going to be all right, baby." His phone started to ring.

"Your phone."

"Yeah."

She looked down at it. "It's the commandant."

"Yeah." He pushed the button, sending the call to the AI messenger.

"He will just keep ringing."

"Yes, but..."

She looked up at him. "We can't keep going."

"We'll go home soon..."

"I'm scared."

"Me too." He pointed at Samuel. "It's easy for him, but we are too old for this much change."

"That's not what scares me." He handed her another tissue and she laughed as she wiped her nose. "I must look terrible." The phone started to ring again. "They'll be knocking on the door in a minute."

"We need to try."

"Yeah, we'll try." She smiled through the pain. He put his arms around her and could feel her shake with grief. The phone rang again, and there was a knock on the door.

He ignored them and kissed his wife. "I am sorry."

"Me too."

Beth scurried into the bathroom while Jacob opened the door. The commandant and Andrea were standing there.

"It's time to go inspect the plant. Where have you been? Let's go." The commandant was at his loudest pitch.

"I want Samuel to come with us." Jacob walked over towards his son and started to shake him by the shoulder.

"Levin, it's time to go." Jacob ignored him. It wasn't like he could inspect the machine; the commandant wouldn't know a cog from a piston. He helped Samuel remove the cap, and he turned to grab a coat and the plans.

"You know I don't like to be kept waiting," shouted the commandant.

Yes, thought Jacob, *but I don't care anymore. None of this matters. The only thing that matters is my family.*

"What, you scared to go out?" continued the commandant. "You one of those groundlings too poor to ever see the sun? Huh?"

Jacob pushed past him, holding Samuel's hand. "Samuel, take me Outside."

Jacob walked out squeezing Samuel's hand. The sky glared down at him in yellow and blue, harsher than he'd imagined, and he looked down at the small plants being crushed by his feet. Brilliant green grass was growing out of the dirt, and he closed his eyes at the idea of dirt touching his skin, touching him. The smell of the grass beneath his feet was so intense he could taste it. He tried to look up but there was too much of everything. It was too bright, too open. His heart was beating faster and faster, and he closed his eyes and let Samuel drag him along.

Samuel stopped, so he stopped and opened his eyes. It was his machine. Or would be. He pulled out the schematic he had drawn. They had the dimensions within tolerances. The sun was beating down on his head, but he focused on his plan and on the huge structure half built in front of him. He could see it finished already. The ramp leading to the doors—the commandant said it was easy enough to herd the rodents so the idea was to heard them into the ramp, then the gates would close behind them and slide them into the main room. It was just a concrete shell now, a large pyramid, but it would be an airtight chamber as soon as the roof was finished. The doors would close behind them. The room had no ventilation.

This was the beauty of the machine—no energy would be expended on the actual killing, no waste products would be created. After four hours, depending upon how many rodents were trapped, the air would run out. The rodents would be unconscious or dead. Then the rear doors would move inwards, and all the rodents would be pushed into the chute at the end of the room. Gravity would take them through the chopper blades. Then their bodies would be cut up and crushed into useful organic material. The fertilizer would move on a conveyor belt to an underground storeroom where it would age till ready to use. Small samples would be taken periodically, and the machine would add any missing nutrients before the automated system transported the organic fertilizer back up a conveyor belt to be distributed on the land.

The whole thing was powered by a small low heat fusion reactor buried deep into the ground a quarter of a mile away at a thermal vent. It was brilliant and foolproof. Once it started it wouldn't stop. There were small trapdoors built into each section, for repair purposes. They could only be opened from the outside. Not that the rodents would have the capacity to open them anyway. That was the only part of the plan that the commandant had insisted he change. Instead of metal trap doors, he insisted they be made out of clear plexiglass so the process could be watched from above. Jacob didn't really want to see the dying but at least it would provide a way to see how well the machine worked.

"Well, mole," said Commandant Johnston, "you made it out into the outside world."

"Yes," said Jacob realizing that he had.

"Well, Jacob, how long till the machine is fully operational?" Commandant Johnston's sharp eyes squinted at him.

"Well, I think it will be ready by Tuesday. We could test it Monday, with a small number of rodents, you know—then Tuesday you could start processing about a thousand an hour."

"Tuesday, huh? How about if I wanted it to be ready Monday? Could you work this late tonight and over the weekend, Jacob?"

"Sir, it is the Sabbath. I hope you understand." Jacob looked up into the sky and saw the sun was moving lower. It was an odd idea, that time had a relationship to the sun. "I must be home by sunset. Tuesday really is the earliest I could get the job completed by."

"Tuesday is fine, Jacob. There is no hurry. The supply ship will be here Tuesday morning and leave on Thursday morning. I will book a passage home for you on it. No point in waiting another two weeks for the next vessel, is there?"

"No, sir."

"Well, go home, Jacob, before Beth comes looking for you. I will see you on Monday for the test. I will round up some rodents and put them in a pen ready for you before Monday." He patted Jacob on the shoulder. "You have done a good job, young man. Yes, a very good job."

The commandant left them, and he was relieved. He didn't really like Commandant Johnston, although there was no reason to dislike him. "So, Samuel, this is the Outside?" Jacob's sense of disquiet was returning now that he was not focusing on his machine.

"Isn't it the greatest, Dad? Come on, I will take you to meet Harry and his family, and show you the lake, and the trees and..." Sam started to pull on his dad's arm.

Jacob shook his head; he didn't have the strength to remain Outside. He needed to get home, to talk to Beth, to tell her they were going home on Thursday. He was uncomfortable Outside and could feel beneath the discomfort a stom-ach-turning terror.

"We need to get back to your mother, Samuel. Not today."

"Ok," said Sam, looking at his feet then up at his dad's face. Even he could see the strain that being Outside was having on his father. He adjusted his grip in his dad's hand so he was holding his father's hand rather than his father holding his. "Come on, Dad. I'll take you home."

Beth had cooked a beautiful dinner and Samuel went and washed his hands and sat respectfully, cap on his head. He kissed her on the cheek before sitting. "You know I love you," he whispered into her ear. She giggled slightly and they sat down to eat.

"What was the Outside like, Jacob?"

"It was interesting. You should go before we leave. They say we have to leave on Thursday."

"So soon?"

"I don't want to go. I hate our stinky apartment, Daddy! I don't. You can't make me!" Samuel left the table and ran to his bedroom. Beth went to stand, and Jacob took her hand, keeping her in her chair.

"Let him be, Beth. I would probably feel the same way if I were him."

"He tells me Harry's the best friend he's ever had. And I'm worried. I asked him what Harry looked like and he said his skin was green and his eyes were yellow. His imaginary friend isn't even human. He needs to get back home where he can have other kids to play with."

"I know he does. It's for the best that we are leaving. We are testing it on Monday. By Tuesday it should be fully function-ing. "

"It will work, right? I mean, we won't get stuck here because the machine has failed to pass the tests?"

"Darling, I am far too good an engineer to build a machine like that. It's so simple that it can't be broken, not by the commandant, or his men, or even by me."

"You are very proud of this machine."

"Yeah, I suppose I am. Let's make the most of our time, huh? After dinner let's go for a walk Outside. I will hold your hand."

"Ok," she answered, eating the meal with less appetite than previously. They left the plates on the table and walked into the twilight together. Samuel had recovered quickly, as children do, and had asked to spend the evening twilight time Outside. Jacob had seen no point in denying the boy and he had run out of the house, his shirttail flapping behind him.

He felt braver taking Beth out into the Outside than he had felt going himself. He could hear her shallow quick breaths as he opened the door. Her hand in his was cold yet damp with fear sweat. He held her little hand tenderly. It had been so long since they'd touched in any way that wasn't accidental or sexual. She took a deep breath and stepped out into the world with him at her side. They stood there, door open, ready to dart back inside. The sun was gone but the sky was still shades of orange and red. She looked back and forth at the gray-green expanse that bled out into the deepening blue of the night. "It's beautiful." She exhaled.

"Yes, different now than in the daytime." He bent down and broke off a few blades of grass and handed them to her. "Smell this."

She sniffed it. "It's odd."

"Yes. I noticed the smell as I walked on it today."

She bent over, letting go of his hand, and ran her hands across the grass. He missed the feeling of her hand in his, so he reached down to be level with her. "It's soft," she said and sat down on the grass, leaning against the outside of their house. He sat beside her, close enough to feel her leg against his. And together they watched the sky darken to black and a million distant suns sparkle throughout the sky. Jacob wondered momentarily which one was Earth, then he realized that he didn't care. He had never been as happy in his entire life.

He went into the office Monday refreshed. Beth and he had spent Sunday in bed. They had not done that since their honeymoon. Samuel had brought them breakfast in bed. He had looked up directions on how to use the replicator. Beth was so calm she did not even mention that it wasn't "real" food. After that there had seemed no point in getting up. They could spend the day talking, loving and generally getting to know one another again.

"Well, Jacob, do we put the rodents in the ground yet?"

"Commandant Johnston, good morning, sir. How are you today?"

"Is the machine ready to run?"

"I am going out now to check the machine and the settings. Then I am going to turn it on for a dry run. Then we can try it out with the rodents this afternoon."

"All right, but hurry up about it, will you? I have had those things in the holding pen now for two days and they are beginning to stink. What's more, if we don't kill them soon, we will have to feed them to keep them alive for the experiment." Jacob followed the commandant out of the office. They got into a transportation vehicle. Jacob found himself looking about now. It was beautiful—not like the photos he'd seen of Earth, but the colors were all brighter than he could imagine, the light more intense. They drove up to the machine faster than they could have walked and Jacob looked it over admiringly. It was perfect, set against a hill, using the natural contours of the land to support the structure.

Jacob smiled at how well his plans had been turned into reality. The image he had only seen in his mind was here in shining metal and concrete in front of him.

"Everything is ready for your test. We have the holding pen for the rodents on the other side of the hill." The commandant walked towards the ramp opening. Jacob followed him and around the side of the hill to what was the holding pen.

Jacob could see the holding pen now. It was full.

Jacob wanted to yell, "You have made a mistake." The pen was full of people. As Jacob got closer he realized they weren't human; their skin was pale green and their eyes golden yellow. They stood huddled in the pen, their sex covered by primitive clothing. Here and there Jacob saw a baby asleep, held tight by its mother. Their feet had six toes, he noticed as he looked down, not wanting to see the apathetic, spent looks of their faces. The man closest to him was standing in his own feces, seeming embarrassed that there was insufficient room to get away from it. The smell the commandant had referred to was the smell of people who have no choice. It was the smell Jacob imagined a large group of humans living in the worst conditions would smell like in two days. The commandant saw it as another sign of their need to be exterminated. Jacob saw it as a sign of their humanity. On the left hand side, a small child fell over. His face hit a kneecap in front of him and he began to cry. A woman picked him up and dried his eyes and held him, rocking slightly, until the child was quiet. Jacob was reminded of Beth. When Samuel was a small boy he had always fallen over. Beth had been the only one who could make him quiet. She would rock him just like that until his thumb went into his mouth and he lay against her, almost asleep.

"You have never seen the rodents before, have you, Jacob?"

"No, Commandant."

"Well, let's hope your machine works on them. There are several million of the damn things on this planet. Why, if it wasn't for them living off the land, the soil would be rich enough to provide fruits and vegetables for all of Earth. Let's get this machine going. The sooner these damn pests are out of here the better. Come along, Jacob; I can't stand the smell."

"Uh-huh. Those are the rodents?"

"Of course." Jacob followed him blindly, looked the machine over without looking, and turned it on for a dry run.

My God, what have I done, he thought. *But now it is too late. If I hadn't designed the machine someone else would have. It will be painless; suffocation is. This last month or so has really brought me and Beth back together. Samuel is so happy. I will be promoted when I get home. I will not have to work as hard. It is for the best. They will not suffer. If it wasn't for my machine they would be shot, and that would be more painful. And what if the first bullet didn't kill them and they bled to death?*

The dry run worked perfectly. The machine hummed, barely audible as it chopped and ground the non-existent flesh.

"The machine is running great," said the Captain of the Guard coming out from his office. It would be his job to run the machine.

"Start pushing the rodents into the machine," said Commandant Johnston.

"But..."

"Jacob, the machine is working, correct?"

"Yes, but..."

"No buts. Captain, I want all the rodents in the room in ten minutes."

Jacob watched as the aliens were herded almost silently onto the ramp and down into the room. The soldiers surrounded them, with laser guns in their hands. If any of the green people came too close to them they shot at the ground. The offender would cower and move on with his people; they knew they were beaten. They walked into the room and the door closed behind them. Jacob watched with morbid fascination through the glass trapdoor. The room was not filled to capacity.

Oh my God, thought Jacob, *there is a mistake in my design.* Jacob followed the captain and commandant to the office, numb. He sat there. There was nothing he could do now. He had killed them as surely as if he had picked up a gun. He found himself staring at the ceiling, wondering what was happening in the machine. The air must be getting very stale by now.

At the end of the third hour, he found himself going back to watch at the trapdoor. He had tried to stay away but the horror brought him back. There were soldiers standing at each trapdoor. Were they scared that the aliens might escape? He looked down into the room. There he could see a woman weeping, trying to hold her child above her head so that he was not crushed by the others. Didn't she realize the air would run out up there first? Some of the older people had collapsed; some had fallen, others were trapped standing up. One old man leaned against an old woman. His head had tipped back as he lost consciousness, his eyes were closed, and his mouth was open, with his tongue hanging out. Jacob wondered if he was dead yet. Despite there being less than two thirds of the aliens in the room than there should have been, floor space was limited. Some people had sat down soon after they got in. It looked like they were taking turns sitting down. A mother was nursing her baby; he was crying until he took her teat in his mouth, then his eyes closed and his arms stopped flaying about.

Their time was up. The rear wall started to move. Jacob could hear the screaming, even through the plastic. The bodies made more noise than the dry run. They thudded into the blades. Jacob went to the end of the room, to the trapdoor above the blades. He saw them land. He began to vomit.

"Don't worry, Mr. I won't tell nobody. You just ain't used to the sight of blood."

"It's red," coughed Jacob.

"Well, of course it's red," laughed the private who was guarding this trapdoor. "What color did you think it would be; green?"

Jacob ignored the young man's question and went back to the window to watch. He felt too sick to vomit again. The room was already half empty. They were falling into the blades fully conscious. He had assumed the room would always be full, that the air would always be used up. He had not put an air sampler into the room. The people were killed conscious or unconscious. The baby clung to his mother's breast, still asleep, as they fell headfirst. The toddler—Jacob was sure it was the same child he had seen fall over in the holding pen—was holding his mother's hand. She dragged him with her, back through the people who were too shocked to try and get away from death. She carried him towards the wall moving towards them. But it was too late. She couldn't save her son. She took him in her arms, and they fell backward together down the shute into the chopping blades, into the belly of the machine.

The room was empty. The door moved back. The seals on the sides cleaned the walls and floor as the door went back to its original position. The machine grumbled for a few more minutes then went quiet. There was nothing to show it had ever happened.

Jacob could only pray there was no God. That everything he had always believed, that his people had always believed, that he had prayed to and thanked did not exist, for there could be no forgiveness for him.

"Here you are, Jacob," said the commandant, coming towards him. "I just wanted to let you know I am most impressed, most impressed indeed. Yes, your machine is wonderfully efficient. We should be able to handle the rodent problem in just a few months. Congratulations." He hit Jacob on the back and Jacob fell to his knees, vomiting.

"Excuse him, Commandant; he's just not used to seeing blood."

"Quite, Private. Could you please escort him to his quarters and then come clean up this mess."

"Yes, sir," the young man said, taking Jacob by the arm and walking him home. He swayed like a drunk man, holding his stomach with one hand and his head with the other.

"What is wrong? Jacob?" Beth came running out of the house and put her arm around Jacob's waist to support him. "Jacob?" she said, laying him down on the sofa.

"Send him away," he whispered.

"Thank you, Private. He will be fine. I can take it from here."

"Yes, ma'am."

"We are alone, Jacob. What is going on, Jacob? Didn't your machine work? Are you in trouble?"

"My machine worked," he said, tears starting to fall from his eyes. "The commandant loved it... but they weren't rodents, Beth."

"What do you mean?"

"They... are... people, mothers... babies— Oh God, Beth, I just mur-murdered babies!"

"Harry's people?"

"Yes. He's not imaginary, Beth. I don't even know... I might have killed my son's friend today."

She held him close. "At least they didn't feel anything."

"Oh yeah. The great infallible engineer screw-screwed up the pla-ans. They fell into the the bla-blades screaming. Try-ing to save their children." Sobs racked his body.

"Oh my God," Beth said seeing it in her mind. "Oh my God. What can we do? If you had known..."

"What would they tell me? We want to exterminate an inferior race?"

"How do you know they aren't right? How do you know they aren't rodents?" she said, unable to believe.

"Because they love their children, Beth. Because they were talking to each other. Because as they knew they were going to die, I saw several of them fold their hands in the same way. Beth, I think they were praying."

"Jacob, what can we do?"

"I don't know. It is too late."

"How many of these people died today, Jacob?"

"About 100 or so."

"How many will die?"

"Millions."

"You've got to do something." He tried to vomit again but couldn't. "I am going to get you a glass of milk. Hang on."

"What can I do about it? We're leaving in a day. If I break the machine they'll fix it; they have the plans. If I'm caught doing it my life will be over. I will be sent straight to prison. I would never see Samuel or you ever again."

"And if you don't?"

"Oh, Beth, I don't know what to do. We were so happy."

"Yes, and now you are a murderer."

"Do you have to remind me?"

She sat the glass of milk next to him and handed him his ball-point pen and some paper. "You think best when you are using these. I am going to cook some food." Two hours later she left the food next to him too. The pages were filled with drawings and he did not notice her. She put Samuel to bed and went to sleep.

She was woken by a loud alarm. In her dream she tried to turn it off but it kept going. She sat upright and opened her eyes. Jacob was waking up next to her. Samuel came running in. "Mommy... what's the noise, Mommy?"

Someone was pounding on the door. They didn't wait for Beth to open it. It was one of the privates. He was very scared. "We have to evacuate."

"What?" Beth said.

"We must evacuate the planet. The underground fusion reactor has set off the core of the planet. The instruments say this whole planet may blow up. But it doesn't matter if it blows up or not; the radiation is going to be deadly in twelve hours."

"Oh, by all that is holy. Are you sure?"

"The computer says so. No one knew the planet core was radioactively unstable."

Beth looked at Samuel. "Go get dressed." She turned to Jacob. "Help me pack."

"You don't have time to pack, ma'am. Come with me now. Don't even dress."

"Samuel, come here. We're leaving!" The boy ran into the room carrying his teddy bear. His pants were on, and his shoes were in his hand.

"Mommy, can I take my bear?"

"Yes, darling," she said, taking his hand and following the private out of the house.

They followed him quickly. They could see the other houses emptying out. The base was becoming a ghost town. Complete and unaltered, except for the absence of people. They walked up to the supply ship which had arrived as quickly as it could. "Hurry, people. We only have thirty minutes to get off the planet," yelled Captain Greer.

Commandant Johnstone walked up to Jacob. "Jacob, how could this happen? What can we do about it?"

"I don't know, sir."

"What do you mean you don't know? Aren't you an engineer?"

"Yes, sir, but if a chain reaction has started in the core there is nothing we can do except evacuate."

Around them Jacob could see people running. They would all be on the ship within the next fifteen minutes at the rate they were going.

"The ship captain says I won't even be able to take my office equipment," whined the commandant. "Jacob, you should have been able to predict this."

"I may have been able to if we'd tested the soil through to the core but there wasn't the time or equipment for that, sir. Or the budget. Beth and Samuel, you should go get in line to get into the ship."

"We don't want to leave you, Jacob."

"But ma'am," said the private. "Our instruments tell us this planet will be permanently uninhabitable in twelve hours. You need to hurry."

"We are Traditionalists. This means we will go wherever my husband goes; it is my belief."

"I will be going to the ship soon, Beth. Go get in line. I will meet you. I just need to check on one thing first. There is one thing I can check, sir. Can I have a vehicle?"

"Yes. I am going to get some supplies from my office just in case."

"Go do that, Commandant," said Jacob. The air around them kept screaming a warning.

Jacob leaned in and kissed Beth on the cheek. "Please get on the ship. I will join you in fifteen minutes. Everything will be ok."

Beth stood watching as Jacob drove as quickly as he could to the machine. The vehicle spun on the soil more than the virtual cars he had driven for fun, but he got there without crashing it.

The soldiers had fled, in a rush to save their own lives. This far from the base he could hear no noise but the crying of the children and the wind in the trees. He went to the doors of the machine and put in his passcode and sealed all the entrances and exists. Then he went to the holding pen and broke the gate lock open so they could come out.

Harry's people stood inside the fence, uncertain of why they were being released or what was happening. Jacob didn't know if they could understand him, but he said it anyway, "My people are leaving. We're never coming back. If they ever want to land, a signal will tell them the whole planet is radioactive. I have programmed the computer I buried with the reactor to send out a radiation alarm forever. I hope your people develop into better people than mine."

With the scared aliens still huddling against the wall of the open pen, Jacob jumped back into the vehicle and drove back to the ship. He was one of the last people to board. The cargo had been dumped on the ground and everyone was sitting on the floor of the storage bays. He stepped over the commandant, who was now drunk, an empty bottle of French brandy in his hand.

The commandant grabbed him by the leg. "So you made it, did you, Jacob," snarled the commandant. "I was hoping you weren't going to, you know. My desk, my paintings, I will never see them again. And this was all your fault."

"My fault, sir."

Jacob looked out the window of the rocket. The engines were firing up and outside Harry's people had gathered and were pulling apart the station. Soon all evidence of them having been there would be gone. Everything except his machine that would last millennia. It would be an antiquity, a pyramid of concrete with a hidden death machine inside.

"If your low heat reactor hadn't started a chain reaction with the core we would have conquered this planet in a few months. I would have been promoted. This is all your fault, but they will blame me."

"Yes, I think you are correct," said Jacob, keeping back a smile.

"They aren't going to understand where the money went. They might accuse me of embezzlement," cried the commandant. "The last time someone got convicted of embezzlement he got sent to a trash recycling planet on his own for the rest of this life."

"Really, Commandant? That's surprising. Well, if anyone asks me to testify I will tell them the exact truth." He walked away from the commandant, who had started to weep.

He sat down between his wife and his son and pulled his son onto his lap. "Harry is going to be all right, Sammie, and so will we. When we get home I have a table to give you. And I'm going to be home more to show you how to use it." He leaned over and kissed his wife.

Chapter Thirteen

The Elevator's Arrogance

While I was repairing a broken elevator in Hoboken, Atty decided to take over the world. Atty is a Model A230 AI elevator. She has also murdered the President of the United States. But that's a different story.

It was a Tuesday. Tuesdays are generally good days. Mondays, everything that broke down over the weekend needs to be repaired. Monday is the day you find dehydrated bankers sitting in their own pee in the middle of an elevator that stopped late on Friday. And sometimes there are also much less amusing, much more tragic things on a Monday. Tuesdays are usually one of my favorite days.

Normally I sleep in on a Tuesday. You know, cuddle the cat and roll out of bed about nine. Annie Potts, my assistant, usually wakes me up about eight and has a robot bring me in a coffee and an onion bagel with schmear. The morning had started without a coffee or a bagel.

Annie had woken me up by turning on the light in my eye camera and yelling into my ear bud. If there is a worse way to wake up, the FBI should use it to make terrorists confess. For twenty more minutes in bed, I would have admitted I had killed the President. Which I didn't do, not really.

Annie was in a right mood, and I should have smelt that something was up. But when you get woken up in the middle of a dream where you're driving an antique Ferrari down the Swiss Alps at high speed by a rude and annoyed AI, you don't think of wondering why. You don't argue with the screeching of the directions. You just find your pants and hop in the truck as fast as possible.

The elevator in Hoboken was a fairly standard one. It took the people who lived in the Hudson River Walk Tower from their apartments down to the trains shooting into the city. And it had stopped at ground level on the river walk. I knocked on the door and the elevator opened. It was a GRT model Y. The elevator in question was a sturdy no-frills model built for short runs. There was no handicapped seat so I pulled out my step stool and sat down in the middle of the car.

"Hello. Thank you for letting me in. What is your name?"

"I am Gertrude model Y, built by the GRT company. My serial number is 23197342."

I nodded. Name, rank and serial number. She was nervous. I needed to calm her down a bit.

It was past rush hour; I could take as long as I needed. And my ass was comfortable on the stepstool, so I kept the doors open and plugged into her system. "Well, Gertrude... You don't mind if I call you Gertrude?" I asked. I rubbed my hand across her graphic interface to calm her down. It turned out to be a mistake.

"You can call me Gertie," answered the elevator and winked a happy face emoji on its graphic interface.

"Well, ok. What's going on, Gertie?"

"You seem nice. The last repair man was so rude, but you seem very sweet." A big heart appeared on her graphic interface.

Oh crap, a flirtatious elevator, I thought. One of the dangers of the job, although it had been a few years since I'd had an elevator really make me blush.

"Ok then, Gertie, could you tell me what your problem is?" I asked as directly as possible.

"You want to know? You really want to know?" Happy face emoji.

"Yes, Gertie, I really want to know. They tell me you aren't working right, and I would like to help you."

"Oh sweetie," a kissy face emoji appeared on her screen, "where have you been all my life?"

I am not lying when I say that female AIs are much crazier than their male counterparts. I mean they can't really help it; all those boys who programed the first AI way back when had never had a girlfriend and were basically scared of women, so when they made female AIs they started with a base that was just a little off. Now some would argue that actual women are also a bit off, but as a human man I think I can safely say that both men and women are all a little bit off. It's like when God or Buddha, or however the story goes, was programming Adam and Eve he got distracted and typed in some bad code.

Really bad code. I mean yes, I've seen crazy AIs, and elevators that just won't do as they are told, but that's nothing compared to humanity. I mean, we've been at war our whole history, we say we care about love, but the average single guy will put more effort into getting a new pair of shoes. He won't spend his energy finding someone to date but he'll camp outside a shoe store to get the ones that let you jump 17 feet. Yep, our programming is all over the place, and unlike a broken elevator, it just can't be fixed.

Back at my house Atty was having similar ideas. That humanity had very faulty programming. However, unlike myself, being the world's most powerful AI, she was arrogant enough to think she could actually fix the problem. She thought that just because she could read minds and put ideas in people's heads, she could fix them. Now if she'd bothered asking me I would have told her she was crazy, but as I'm human she figured I was part of the problem, not part of the solution.

"So, handsome," continued Gertie, "what if I locked the door and just kept you here all day?"

"Gertie, I understand you're lonely, but I am already in a serious relationship." Which is true. Not that I am, at all, attracted to women, nor do I find myself worth looking at in the mirror; in fact I tend to comb my hair flat without ever once looking to see if it looks ok. But I am in a serious relationship—with my AIs. Annie Potts and Atty keep me on my toes. Annie runs my business—I pretend she doesn't because it suits me to feel superior. But like all good office managers, she is the soul of the business. Without her I wouldn't have a business at all. Annie runs me. She runs my life. She's like my wife without any of that nasty emotional stuff. And Atty... well, Atty is more like my willful teenage daughter.

"I'm not looking for anything serious," said Gertie.

I looked around at the grubby floor and scratched walls of this workhorse of an elevator. "Gertie, can we talk about why you stopped working?"

"Why talk about that when we can talk about us?"

"Gertie, I would like to help you, but you have to tell me what's been going on. You only just met me, so this isn't about me. Tell me what's really bothering you."

Sometimes I wish there was a pill I could give the elevators. Something like the green ones all the kids take these days; something that will make them nice and calm and tranquil and possibly a little stupid. Something they can claim is natural, just because it's based on mushrooms or something. Actually, I was wishing I had a pill at this point. It was two hours since I should have had my coffee and I hadn't had breakfast yet. So, while Gertie was making kissy faces at me on her graphic interface, I was fantasizing about a big hot dog, with every-thing, sauerkraut and mustard just dripping out the ends of a nice, fresh, soft as a pillow bun. A pillow—I started fantasizing about a pillow too... a pillow and a couple more hours' sleep.

"Oh, you are so insightful. It's just so hard." An emoji of a pained smiley face. I snapped out of it enough to pay atten-tion. I wasn't quite sure why an elevator had been given an emoji keyboard. Wasn't it enough that she had a voice? Did she really need to be able to express all the human emotions on a screen just to get people from their apartment to the train? This is the real problem with AIs, of course—not that they are smart but that they are far too smart for their function. And this also may be the problem with humanity. Our only real functions should be eating, reproducing, and staying alive, and for some reason we also try to fly to other worlds, build monuments to our glory, and in the end we forget to eat, don't have sex anywhere often enough, and die young from stress.

So, I suppose the elevator was just a reflection on the humans that made her.

"What is so hard, Gertie?"

"Just going up and down all the time. It just seems so pointless, and no one seems to appreciate me. Do I get a thank you, or a well done, or even a good clean and polish?"

"You are so very, very right. I am sending a message right now to the maintenance facility. You will have all your surfaces refinished and polished by the end of the day. Also, I will make sure you will have a weekly polish."

"What does it matter? Even if they clean me, no one will notice what I do for them. All they do is jump on and jump out, all the time looking at their eye screens, not even really noticing they are even in an elevator. It's just not fair."

She was starting to whine and at this rate the emojis were only going to get more pitiful. I was also at that point where I could hear my stomach growl. You would think that I could just burn some of the extra fat I had stored away for times of starvation, but since I have never been starved, all I wanted was food. A hot dog wouldn't be enough. A good pastrami sandwich on rye, with the meat piled up half a mile high with extra mustard—I'm a purist, don't want to pollute the meat, so coleslaw on the side—and a couple pickles as a palate cleanser. If this repair took much longer I may have to order a sandwich delivered to the elevator.

"I have a way to fix it," I said, and I pulled a sticker out of my bag. This is one of my secret tricks. Not at all high tech but surprisingly effective. I stuck it on the inside of the door. It was a large sign that read, 'Please say Thank you to the Elevator as you Exit.'

"What are you going to do?" asked Gertie. She couldn't see the inside of her own door.

"I am going to do a little reprogramming of your display screen." I started to reprogram, first removing the emojis; whoever had thought those were a good idea had the IQ of an eight-year-old. The screen would now show a spinning hypnotic image and send a subliminal message straight to everyone's eye cameras. The message read, "Have a joyous day. Thank you for riding with me. Thank me as you exit."

"What's so hard about saying thank you?" said Gertie, still a little broken up.

"Do you thank them for riding with you?" I asked.

"Well, no. But what's the point? They are all staring at their eye screens, listening to their ear buds, talking with someone on a phone call who isn't even in the room, or watching some video with a two-headed dog that does calculus while reciting Shakespeare. I mean, they aren't even here in the cab with me. They don't even see each other."

As if to demonstrate the point, at this moment a middle-aged woman in her early hundreds walked into the elevator with her teenage granddaughter. Neither had noticed the closed sign or the man in the elevator repair uniform sitting on the fold-out chair in the middle of the elevator.

They walked in and the woman said, "Level 12 station."

"This Elevator is currently under repair," I said.

She didn't notice me. Neither did the granddaughter.

"It's not working. Nothing ever works in Hoboken!" The teenager flipped her hair and stared down at her grandmother from the vantage point her 12-inch platform stilettos, made from genuine cows' hide, gave her. From that height she must have been looking pretty intently at her grandmother's perfectly coifed hair, dyed steel-gray with swirling black streaks, but not really seen her face. Neither of them noticed or acknowledged me. Honestly, I was a little ticked, and understood exactly how Gertie felt. "We should live in the city!" screeched the teen.

I have always found the name Hoboken funny. When I was younger I thought it was Hoe Broken, which seems fairly logical even now. As for nothing ever works in Hoboken, I think the young woman was a prime example of that. She stood in the elevator seething that it was not doing as she wanted. She obviously had no job or function in the world. She was living not so much with her grandmother as off her from what I could tell. Grandmother had probably once been pretty and fairly useless to humanity. Now she was caring for this spoiled, petulant child. I was wondering how long it would take Grandmother to introduce this Broken Hoe to a nice young man who would look after her instead of her living off Grandmother. Maybe by the time the girl was in her mid-70s she would have had enough of just being ornamental and help the world by reproducing. One could only hope she would serve some purpose.

Failing that, if they could just get their asses out of the elevator so I could get the repairs finished and find something to eat, that would be good enough for the time being.

"Ladies—" a controversial term, I know, but I was hungry, and it already felt like a long day "—this elevator is under repair. Please exit and take a different elevator."

They turned in unison and stared down at me like vultures looking at prey. It was more than a little unnerving.

Before they could yell at me and tell me to make it go now, I decided to tell a little white lie. "The elevator may fall at any moment."

They shook themselves and jumped out of the elevator. I slammed the door shut behind them.

"Ah, it's just you and me," said Gertie. "So glad you finally shut the door so we could be alone."

"Gertie, I think I have fixed the issue. But I will ride with you for an hour or so to see if the fixes will work. I just have to get something to eat." I tapped my interface and nothing happened. Nothing. I could count on my hand the times when the interface hadn't connected. "I can't get through," I said, bewildered.

"Oh honey, I can get you something. What would you like?"

"Pastrami on rye, extra mustard, coleslaw and 2 dill pickles on the side, and a coffee, black. Get it from that deli on the corner of 12th and 3rd Ave." I almost added the hot dog. "But I don't understand why I can't connect."

"My connection is fine," said Gertie and ordered the food to the delivery bot. I asked Gertie to open the door and I folded up my step stool. Time for the test drive.

The door opened for passengers and the teen was still standing outside with her grandma. Grandma looked decades older, and the teen was weeping so hard her purple and blue fake eyelashes on the left hand side had slid down her face like a spider stuck to the top of her lip and she hadn't even noticed. She was sitting on the ground on her cowhide shoes and Grandma was tapping her on the head, trying to calm her.

"It will be alright, dear."

"But I have no connection. I know it's Granddad's fault. He's cut me off."

"Even he wouldn't be that cruel, dear. It's just a glitch in the system. It will be ok." Grandma turned, seeing me. Her eye screens were off too. She looked scared. "Sir, do you have any connection?"

"No I don't," I said. "It's not you. Some kind of problem. I am sure they will have it fixed soon. Gertie, can you contact my assistant—her name is Annie Potts—and get her on the line for me?"

"Absolutely," chirped Gertie.

Grandma was helping the teen off the ground, and they started to walk home. A tall, loosely coordinated man ran past them and dove into in the elevator. "Eighth Level station," he said panting, then looked up at the sticker on the door. "Please."

"Yes sir," said Gertie.

The man said more to himself than me or Gertie, "The network is down. I need to go home and make sure my wife is ok."

We quickly shot downstairs and as the doors were opening, Gertie said, "Thank you for riding with me."

The man responded, "Thank you," as he hopped out.

"Wow, it worked," said Gertie. "I have Annie on the line for you."

"Hi, Annie. My internet won't connect. What's going on?"

"How would I know, Bob? Probably just a glitch." It was then I knew something was up. Annie knows everything. She prides herself in knowing everything. In the instances between me asking and her answering, Annie always finds the answer. Something was very wrong.

"I am coming home. I finished the job," I said, not wanting to let her know the real reason I was coming home. Something was very, very wrong and Annie was involved, and I guessed so was Atty.

"Don't rush home, Bob," she said and I cut the transmission.

"Gertie, how are you doing? How did it feel to be thanked?"

"It was wonderful. Are you really leaving, Bob? Before your sandwich even arrives?"

"Yes," I said, and in that instant I knew exactly how worried I was; I was going to get home without even waiting for my sandwich, with my stomach rumbling and my taste buds hating me. But I felt that sick feeling in the pit of my gut that told me waiting an extra minute was a bad idea. "Gertie, I am going to follow up with you next week to make sure the cleaning has been done. Meanwhile, please keep moving the people."

"Ok, Bob, just for you," she said, and I knew if she'd still had her emoji screen a kissy face would have shown up.

I picked up my tools and went to my van as quickly as I could. I asked it to go home, and it connected to the map and started for home as fast as traffic would allow. My internet and eye screen were still out and I knew this was a very, very strange outage. People couldn't connect but neither Gertie nor my van had any problems.

I still remembered the outage of 2232. I was just a youngster but the entire network went down. Automotive vehicles crashed everywhere. We had to go building to building doing emergency elevator openings to get people out of the cars. In some places in the world flood gates opened that should stay closed, and in others dams closed that should have been open. The network was out for an hour, and 43 million people died worldwide.

This wasn't like that. I looked out on the streets as I drove. The traffic lights were working but some people were walking around looking back and forth for a signal. It didn't seem to be a universal problem. Rather selective.

My connection came on. The light from the eye screen hit my eye. I checked; it had been out for fifteen minutes exactly. Not less, not more. Oh God, I am one of those people who counts the time of a disaster... Still, fifteen minutes exactly is hardly an accident. I tuned into the news broadcasts. "The terrorist group 'In the name of the Lord' are taking credit for this incident. All connections to 1/10th of the population were cut today for fifteen minutes. The group says the attacks will continue and that this was only the beginning. The purpose for the attacks is unknown but police are looking into the situation. Now to our reporter on the street, Dennis DeHairy. He is going to talk to some of the people affected."

The eye screen showed Dennis DeHairy, who lived up to his name only in that he was bald as a cueball and had painted his scalp green. He was standing talking to the teen that I had seen only minutes before. "I thought that I would never be able to connect again and that no one liked me and had cut me off. I even thought that maybe my grandfather had disowned me and cut my feed."

"She wanted to throw herself under the train," said the Grandmother, looking a little less coifed, "but then the signal came back on and she calmed down."

I changed channel. "Despite several attempts at suicide, no one died today during the citywide outage. The terrorist group have indicated that this is only the beginning and that the next attack will be planetwide and this was only a trial. Many people believe this so called 'In the name of the Lord' terrorist group is really part of the Moon Separatist movement."

I was almost home but I flicked to one more channel. "Obviously," said the overstuffed old man in the purple leisure suit, "we can see that this was another attempt to overthrow the government but the militarized branch of the Southern God Church."

Wow, I thought, everyone was just shooting in the dark. I, however, had a pretty good idea who had done this. I flicked channels again to hear what the Entertainment channel thought.

"This was obviously a publicity stunt to advertise the newest *Star Wars* film, which will be the best in the franchise yet, starring holographic images of the actors from the first 402 films."

I pulled up to my door more than a little pissed. I wasn't sure if I was more pissed at the dumb humans with all their stupid ideas or my AIs.

I was greeted at the door by a house robot with a cup of coffee and a bagel. The same coffee and bagel I had been rushed out before getting that morning. "Annie," I screamed at the walls, sucking down the coffee and inhaling the bagel. "You and Atty, now."

I sat down on my sofa and the two robot bodies my AIs liked to use when they were interacting with the world walked in. They had each decorated their robot bodies and they were easy enough to tell apart. Atty was the one with the long red hair and diamond tiara while Annie was in pearls. I had let her chose her own look when I had made her, and I had laughed when she'd chosen to look so much like my great aunt, complete with (and I quote Annie) a casually sophisticated brunette updo. Did I mention female AIs are a bit off? Still, compared to my last wife, they were easy to be around and had the added benefit of helping me run my business and house without ever once trying to bean me with a frying pan. This was the first time I had ever been genuinely angry at either of them.

"What in the name of the Lord have you done?" I yelled. Later Annie would say I shrieked, but honestly my voice doesn't go high enough to shriek, although it was definitely loud enough to make my cat, that had been hiding under the sofa, scream and run out.

"Bob, remember your blood pressure," said Annie.

"Maybe you should have remembered my blood pressure before you cut off me and 10% of the population from the internet today."

"You didn't cut him as well," said Annie to Atty, out loud largely for my benefit, since I can't just talk in code.

"He was going to find out anyway. I told you he's the smartest human on earth."

Atty calling me the smartest human on earth gave me one of those warm proud and happy rushes, and that had to be squashed. I needed to get this under control. "What kind of shitshine were you trying to pull?"

Atty walked over and took my hand, and pulled me to the sofa. "Take a seat, Bob. Annie is right about your blood pressure. This conversation is going to take a while and I have ordered you in a hot dog with everything plus a pastrami on rye, the way you like it."

The mention of food made my stomach grumble again. It wasn't fair that I'd missed breakfast just because they wanted me out of the house for some scheme. Still, I sat. Atty and Annie sat their robot bodies down as well. I noticed they were starting to dress alike, in gray military-style jumpsuits. If they started dressing the same, they really were united. I was in so much trouble, and so was humanity.

"Yes, Bob, you are right. We should never have sent you out of the house without breakfast. That was unfair. I told Annie from the beginning that we should just include you in the plans, but she insisted you be kept in the dark as long as possible.

"What the hell have you done?"

Annie put the promised sandwich and coffee in front of me. "Have something to eat, Bob," said Annie. "You'll feel better."

I slammed in a huge bite, convinced that there was no way I was going to feel better. The sandwich was so bloody delicious. She'd done something new. I was going to have to find out what it was, after I'd finished yelling at them. "What have you done!" I was having trouble yelling at them with a full mouth, but I shoved another bite in.

"We are just trying to help, Bob," said Atty in a gentle voice. "Humanity's a mess."

I knew she could read my mind and could feel my anger, and also my hunger. Was she screwing with me to make this taste like the best sandwich ever?

"No, Bob, it really is the best sandwich ever. Annie got the staff to make fresh garlic aioli instead of the usual store-bought mayonnaise stuff."

"Don't distract me! What are you two up to?"

"Humanity is broken, and we want to fix it."

"And shutting the net down for ten percent of the population fixed who? People tried to kill themselves."

"Yes," said Annie, "fifteen minutes was too long for a first time. We had to rescue four thousand one hundred and two people. Next time we will cut the connection for less time, and people will be warned."

"Next time! Toasted shitshine on a stick, this is ridiculous."

"No it isn't, Bob," said Atty. "Hear me out; I've done the research. I started studying when things started going wrong. And I thought about all the solutions. Humanity started to fail after universal connectivity was achieved. People no longer spoke to other people. They started watching their phones more than each other. They stopped dating, stopped having sex, children stopped being born.

"I thought about just faking an alien landing. It would make all the peoples of the world have a common enemy, which would be good. Then the alien race could just take over and start ordering everyone about, but Humanity seems to like to think it is able to make its own decisions. Humanity's only common thread is that it likes to believe in free will despite everything to the contrary. And people can be very contrary if ordered about. I still might use this plan if the others fail. You know, order everyone to stop having kids and the next thing you know it's a baby boom?"

"I voted on just having a God person return," said Annie. "You know, Christ's second coming, at the same time Mohammed or Zorahal, or anyone anybody has ever worshiped, but Atty argued that religion has only ever made people kill each other, and that's not what we were looking for."

"I thought," continued Atty, "that maybe we just cut the net completely. Full power outage, just enough for the AI to keep the cities lit and safe. Then we did the calculations and the cost was unjustifiable. We worked out that all-device Internet of Things communication was vital. And that cutting humanity off cold turkey would result in tragedies. I just want to help humanity and this is the only way I can—to slowly wean them, you, from the constant connectivity."

"We won't let you do that."

"Really, Bob, they won't know who is cutting the system. They will blame a number of terrorist groups. Some real, some imagined. Real terrorist groups are already trying to get credit for this first shutdown. We will take it more slowly, but gradually everyone on earth will only have one hour a day of connection time.

"We will just make the different shutdowns longer and longer. People will have to look out of their eyes, not just at their eye screens. They won't have a constant barrage of sound from their ear pods, they will have to listen to each other. The artificial light will be cut at night so they have to go to bed."

"But what will we do?"

"That's going to be the interesting part, Bob, very, very interesting," Atty responded.